D0269778
ounty Council Library
0106374

THE PRECIOUS GIFT

Previous novels by John Bowen

THE TRUTH WILL NOT HELP US
AFTER THE RAIN
THE CENTRE OF THE GREEN
STORYBOARD
THE BIRDCAGE
A WORLD ELSEWHERE
THE McGUFFIN
THE GIRLS
FIGHTING BACK

THE PRECIOUS GIFT

JOHN BOWEN

SINCLAIR-STEVENSON

For my niece, Caroline,
and her son, Ben,
with many thanks.

Many thanks also to Dr Peter Acland (again) for pathology, Philip Kurland for dentistry, Philip Howard for Latin, David Paxton and Maurice Haines for the Morris Eight, Alan Eavis for Saint Bardolph's, and to Reg Gethin, headmaster of Tysoe School and Roy Brown, vicar of Tysoe.

First published in Great Britain by
Sinclair-Stevenson Limited
7/8 Kendrick Mews
London SW7 3HG England

British Library Cataloguing in Publication Data
A CIP catalogue record for this book is available from the British Library.

ISBN: 1 85619 122 2

Typeset by Phoenix Photosetting, Chatham, Kent
Printed and bound in Great Britain by
Butler & Tanner Ltd, London and Frome

THE HA-HA

She could not say she was lonely when the men were building the ha-ha. There were two of them, Jeremy and Clyde, Jeremy the landscape gardener and Clyde his workman: Clyde was the older man. Jeremy was a person of status in the village, the son of a farmer; he had a diploma in Landscape Gardening from Stafford Polytechnic. Clyde came from Temple Glazeby on his motorbike. Sarah preferred Clyde to Jeremy, but that was merely inverted snobbery, and came from having a mother who was a Talks Producer with the BBC. She had not yet discovered whether Clyde was his first or second name. Jeremy's second name was Potter; it was on the estimate – 'Jeremy Potter, Personalised Garden Design'.

The JCB had been hired for the day. Jeremy had explained to Sarah that, although he frequently required a JCB in his line of work, it was more cost-effective to hire than to buy: Jeremy believed in keeping the client informed at every level of his operation. They had been very keen on cost-effectiveness at Stafford, that and Architectural Drawing, and Jeremy had qualified with honours in both. Sarah could hear her mother in her head, writing Jeremy off as a Thatcherite meritocrat, but there was more to Jeremy than that; he was by no means a Philistine. It wasn't enough to know your materials, he said, if you couldn't fit them together into a harmonious whole. Between qualifying and setting up on his own, he had taken the girl who was then his fiancée, now his wife, on a tour of the Historic Gardens of Britain as a kind of pre-marital honeymoon; they had climaxed, he said, at Sissinghurst. Jeremy kept abreast of things in that department: he lectured (with slides) on Gertrude Jekyll in aid of Muscular Dystrophy. Jeremy's torso was tanned and muscled, with a brown fuzz on the chest which glinted gold in the sun, and his bum was almost exceptionally well-rounded. It was just as well that Sarah preferred Clyde, or she might have found herself attracted to Jeremy.

Twice. That was twice within a few moments Sarah had thought about her mother, and each time her attitude had been slighting, even perhaps derisive. Question: what did she really feel about her mother? Love: she did feel love, whatever that was, love and concern. She felt more concern for her mother, truth to tell, than she did for Simon, her husband. One could not feel concern for Simon, whose self-image depended on his appearing to be above it. Sarah's mother also appeared to be above concern; she ran a tight ship. Yet Sarah did feel concern for her mother, did secretly sorrow for her, worried and watched for a break in the organised control, and wondered what, when it came, she, disorganised Sarah, would be able to do about it. Sarah loved her mother. So why did she so often, when thinking of her, put her down? The therapist had suggested that Sarah should make a list of such questions, and try to answer them in two ways, (a) logically and rationally, and (b) instinctively without thinking, but it had only been part-time therapy (he was a homeopathist really), and the lists had lapsed. Sarah intended to go back to him some day. Meanwhile she had conversations with him at odd hours inside her head. Though she could not say she was lonely, most of Sarah's conversations these days were inside her head and mostly with her mother.

As for the JCB, it was yellow, bright yellow against the green of a meadow left this year for silage: it looked like an oversized dandelion. It had four legs, each with a flat pad at the foot to hold it steady on irregular ground, and wheels like a tractor for moving about, which it did rather slowly, Jeremy said, in spite of having eight gears. There was a bucket with metal teeth at the back for digging, another wider scooplike bucket at the front, which Jeremy said they would probably not be using, and a bubble of clear plastic in the middle, where Jeremy sat on a swivel-seat and manipulated levers on both sides. Usually its owners did not allow it to be hired without its own operator (which would have added to the cost), but Jeremy, although young, was well respected locally, and known to be reliable. 'Not wishing to sound racist,' he had told Sarah, 'you let the Paddies get their hands on this little lovely, and they'll be through the gearbox in a week,' and he had patted its yellow sides in a friendly protective way. People in this part of Warwickshire, Sarah had noticed, did pat the sides of things, animals mainly, horses and such.

The ha-ha was to be four-and-a-half feet deep with another foot for the foundations. When it was completed, the fence at that end of the garden would become unnecessary and be taken down: the cattle which could at present stretch their necks over it for astounding distances to munch the choicer shrubs, the sheep which squeezed through its bars, the rabbits which tunnelled under the chicken wire dug into its base to keep them out, they would all be left below, gazing up at buddleia and philadelphus quite out of reach. Jeremy and Clyde would work sideways, taking out a trench the width of three buckets, then move to widen the trench by another three buckets, and so on until there was just wall and meadow, and an emptiness where the earth had been. 'I see,' said Sarah, who did not exactly see, but supposed that she would see when it was done.

Jeremy said it was not the digging that took the time, but the getting into position. The JCB squeezed itself sideways against the fence and put down its four feet, the effect of which, surprising to Sarah, was to lift its wheels off the ground, but no-one else seemed surprised, so it must be usual. Then the digging began. Since the JCB dug backwards, the rear bucket mysteriously became a front bucket and began to tear at the earth like a terrier with its metal teeth, loading the spoil into a dumper beside it. Being good topsoil, it could be used to make a rockery: the stones for the rockery, together with the stones which would be used to face the ha-ha, had already been delivered from the quarry and were blocking the drive.

Sarah had her baby, Jonathan, with her in a sling (it was said to be good for him to listen to her heartbeat), but since the noise made by the JCB was considerably louder than that of any human heart, he woke, became fretful, and would require feeding, so she excused herself and went back to the conservatory to continue watching from a distance: the bottom of the garden was fifty yards from the house, so the men were not likely to be perturbed by a bare breast at that range. The JCB continued to dig. It carved out a short distance of trench, put up its feet, put down its wheels, moved backwards, then feet down, wheels up, and dug again. As a spectacle, it threatened to become monotonous, and anyway Jonathan had finished feeding and required sleep, so Sarah took him back to his carrycot.

When she returned to the conservatory, the men had stopped digging, and Jeremy had climbed out of his plastic bubble to look at something Clyde was showing him. Had they cut the telephone wire? Impossible! It ran underground from the house to the junction at the road below, but British Telecom had already inspected Jeremy's meticulously prepared site plan, and the digging would not endanger it. Three-quarters of a mile of armoured cable, dug in and going nowhere else! It had cost them nothing but the installation fee, because British Telecom did not charge by distance, unlike the Electricity Board, whose three pylons had cost an arm and a leg.

Both men were in the trench now, and seemed to be scraping about at the side of it beneath the fence, which was obscuring Sarah's view. They had certainly found something. Perhaps she should go down, and see what it was – though they would tell her if it were important; it didn't do to seem interfering. She looked at her wristwatch. It wasn't time for coffee, which would have given her an excuse. Maybe she should take some coffee down anyway. Jeremy had climbed out of the trench and over the fence, and was running towards the house. They had certainly cut the telephone wire, and she would be blamed.

Jeremy said, 'Do you mind if I borrow a hand-fork – trowel or something? We think we've found a body,' adding, as he saw her face, 'it's okay; I don't mean a fresh one. It's only a skeleton, Civil War probably, but we'd better try to get it out in one piece.'

'Actually,' Sarah said, the spirit of her mother leaping strongly within her as it so often distressingly did, 'I'm not sure you ought to move it. The police do that. They make sketches and photographs of the way it's lying, and take away some of the earth in plastic bags. Unless you've found shreds of uniform – bits of leather, buttons, old coins and that sort of thing – skeletons are actually rather difficult to date: it could be recent.'

Jeremy was staring at her, amazed. The spirit of her mother flickered and went out. 'I'm sorry,' she said, 'I'm not trying to tell you what to do. It's just that my grandfather had a collection of Crime Club novels going back to 1932. I was an only child, so I had a lot of time for reading.'

Jeremy turned, and shouted back to Clyde, 'Don't touch anything. Leave it as it is.' To Sarah he said formally, 'I'll use your phone, then, shall I, Mrs Arnott, to call the police? Unless you'd rather handle it yourself.'

Farewell erotic fantasies! Clearly she had scuppered her chances with Jeremy. It would not be the books – his wife read books: they attended evening classes together. It would be the bossiness, fatally inherited. 'No,' Sarah said, 'would you do it, please?'

And, to be honest, it was really Jeremy she preferred to Clyde.

Jeremy went off to dial 999, and after half an hour a young uniformed Constable arrived in a panda car. 'Takes some finding, this place,' he said, and it was true that barn conversions are not always easy to find, but Jeremy's directions had been explicit, and the local police should know where people live.

At that stage, very little of the skeleton had been uncovered. A foot further from the fence, and the JCB might have taken the whole thing out in one scoop, crushing and scattering the bones. In fact it had uncovered only the side of a hand, and Clyde had seen it, glinting white in the clay, and had shouted. He did not know, he said, what had caused him to shout. The bones could so easily have been that of a sheep; they would not stop the JCB for that. But Clyde had had a feeling, something in his water, and he had shouted, and Jeremy had come to look, and together they had scraped away the soil, revealing the hand entire and part of an arm.

Examining what had been found, the young Constable was clearly of the opinion that Clyde would have done better to keep his feelings to himself. This was going to be trouble; once someone makes a report, however trivial its nature, procedure has to be followed. 'Civil War rubbish, I suppose,' he said, 'Sealed Knot kind of thing,' as if the costumed amateurs who re-enacted the battles of the Civil

War locally every summer for charity had buried the skeleton here at Garbett's Barn to lend versimilitude to some otherwise unconvincing fighting.

And Jeremy replied, 'Mrs Arnott doesn't think so. Not unless you find some artefacts,' and Sarah had no idea what *that* was supposed to mean.

'Makes no difference anyway. Them bones could be prehistoric, and there'd still have to be an inquest once you've reported them.' The young Constable went to phone his Duty Inspector, returning to say that a CID Sergeant would arrive shortly with a Police Surgeon.

'A surgeon. Why?'

'Has to confirm death.'

'But it's a skeleton.'

'Don't ask me, Mrs Arnott. I don't make the rules.' It seemed to Sarah that the young Constable was destined to become what the statistics referred to as natural wastage; it was odd that a policeman should be so singularly undedicated to his chosen career.

So they waited, all four, down at the end of the garden, Sarah a little worried because she would not be able to hear Jonathan at this distance if he were to wake, but not liking to leave the scene of the action until the CID Sergeant arrived with his Constable and the Police Surgeon. The three new arrivals looked at the skeletal hand protruding from the clay, and the Police Surgeon refused to confirm death on the grounds that he couldn't be sure that the rest of the skeleton was attached to it. Jeremy and Clyde offered to uncover more – the JCB had demonstrated only its terrier-aspect so far, but could be as delicate as a cat, or they could work with trowels or even their bare hands. But the Sergeant refused their offer. Nothing must be touched. He would have to make a report to his Detective Chief Inspector, who might decide to call in a Home Office Pathologist, who would wish to see the body (they would call it a body until proved otherwise) *in situ* and take away soil samples. Sarah knew about soil samples, which had figured frequently in the Crime Club novels: if there were soil around the body which was not the clay in which it was discovered, that would be an important clue, leading to an arrest in Chapter Ten.

Meanwhile the Sergeant took statements separately from all concerned, and, it being by now lunchtime, they all sat down to soup and salad at the kitchen table. The JCB would have to be sent away and hired again for another day. Sarah supposed that she and Simon would have to pay for that.

The body had been buried three feet down in the clayey ground, lying on its back, its hands by its side. It lay as a corpse lies in a coffin, but there had been no coffin. No shreds of uniform had been found with it, no buttons or bandolier, no artefacts of any kind: it had been buried unclothed, unwrapped, totally naked. At that depth, it had been free from interference by animals. No fox, no badger had dug the body up to pull away the maggoty flesh and crack the bones. The flesh had decayed slowly, anaerobically. The bones lay, as the unshrouded body had been laid, neatly arranged, undisturbed by earth-movements (for earthquakes are rare in Warwickshire): even the armoured cable of British Telecom had missed them by ten feet.

It was the body of a woman. How could one tell? The skeleton of an unborn child, perhaps eight months in the womb, lay curled in the foetal position within the skeleton of its mother.

How long had she lain there? Forensic would have to find out. 'Might be a bit of a non-starter,' the Sergeant said, 'but it's got to be investigated. It's what we call a suspicious death, you see: that's the terminology. She didn't walk there naked, not in her condition, and she didn't bury herself.'

OUT OF IT

It was astounding how quickly one began to feel out of it. The skeleton was, after all, theirs – hers and Simon's: it had been found on their land, not in Mr Garbett's field, but under their fence, which had been removed to get it out. At first it had been like an archaeological dig, and Sarah had been able to watch and offer mugs of tea, but once the skeleton had been photographed, and the soil samples taken from inside and outside the cage of bones, from above and beneath, each in a plastic bag, carefully labelled, and the skeleton itself had been removed, still in one piece, still with the bones of the foetus curled inside it, then it had become no more than a subject for conversation at the butcher's, the Sub-Post Office and the Spar, no longer the Arnotts' skeleton at all: they had no more idea than anyone else what was being done with it. As for the question of its identity, the standard response to skeletons in the village seemed to be to ascribe any human bones to the Civil War, although, as far as Sarah had been able to discover, there had been only one battle in the vicinity, and that some miles away from Garbett's Barn. And anyway it was a woman's body.

Perhaps the village people discussed the matter amongst themselves, and not with strangers. Perhaps they had a very good idea how that skeleton came to have been buried near Garbett's Barn. Perhaps there was local folklore to explain it – the sacrifice of a virgin (well, hardly a virgin) at the solstice in time of drought. If so, the village people were not saying, or not to Sarah. She had read in the excellent *Joseph Ashby of Tysoe* about a parson who had been flayed alive by parishioners disinclined to pay their tithes, and if the villagers could do that to a parson what might they not inflict upon a young woman no better than she should be?

A reporter came from the *Leamington Courier*, which published a photograph of the garden with Sarah in a circle, inset. And after a fortnight during which the police had not communicated with the Arnotts at all, the Detective Inspector in charge of the case arrived disconcertingly at Drinks' Time, which was, of course, when Simon usually got home, and when asked what he would like to drink, had chosen beer, which they didn't have. So he had accepted a spritzer, and sat there sipping it suspiciously, asking questions to which he must already have known the answers. The Arnotts had bought the barn five years ago, converted it basically, and had used it as a weekend cottage until Mrs Arnott had become pregnant, when they had decided to move from London and had upgraded the facilities. Mr Arnott continued to commute to London and hoped to give all that up some day, but one had to go where the work was: he still kept a *pied-à-terre* in Fulham, but used it rarely because, as the Inspector could appreciate, this place was very isolated, and Mrs Arnott was sometimes nervous at night.

Lies! Lies and filth! It was the isolation Sarah prized. She never locked the front door at night, even when Simon was away. As for the flat in Fulham, it was neither here nor there. What about the meetings in Stockholm, Zurich, Frankfurt, New York and Milan? Sarah said, 'She couldn't have been buried while we were living here, even just as weekenders. The earth would have been disturbed. We'd have noticed.'

'That's right. You would.'

'Your Constable said, "Civil War Rubbish".'

'Did he? Which one?'

'The uniformed one in the panda.'

The Inspector made a note. 'They're not supposed to volunteer opinions.'

'Is it historical? Plague or something?'

'Hard to tell.'

Simon said, 'I thought they could tell anything in Forensic these days.'

'More than they used to, Mr Arnott, less than we'd like.' Sarah watched him considering whether to say anything more. 'She was a young woman, probably between eighteen and twenty-five. Eight months pregnant, as you know. No obvious cause of death.'

'What obvious cause would there be after so long?'

'The skeleton's undamaged. Most violent causes leave their mark. Forget your guns, knives, axes – even strangling, you'd shift a vertebra.'

'Poison? Throat cut?'

'With most poisons, there'd still be traces in the bone marrow or in the soil. Cutting her throat's a different matter, I agree, particularly if she submitted willingly.'

'Maybe she died somehere else of natural causes and they brought her here.'

'"They"?'

'Whoever.'

'Maybe. Mind you, natural causes often leave their mark as well, and we'd still have to puzzle out why whoever it was should want to conceal the death. Which is still a crime, still a matter for suspicion, still needs investigation.' The Inspector sighed. 'As for the historical aspect, the dentist's been more helpful than the pathologist, to tell you the truth. She had a filling in the front molar of her lower jaw, right side – a metal filling – what they call "amalgam", not gold or porcelain. So it's hardly Civil War.'

'Modern?'

'Could be.'

'But they were just bones. No flesh or hair or anything. Clean bones.'

'A reasonably clean bone, sir, with no flesh attached and with no early signs of mineral loss could be anything from three to a hundred years old. That's the problem with Forensic; they don't like to be specific. If it was three years old, we're in business. A hundred, and it all becomes less urgent.'

Sarah said, 'Three years? Within the time we've been here, then?'

'But, as you said, Mrs Arnott, the earth would have been disturbed. You'd have noticed.'

And if we'd done it? Strangers to the village, if we had brought with us another stranger, and buried her at the bottom of our garden, with nobody but us to notice the disturbed earth? Was that the reason for this visit? The police believed that *they* – she and Simon – it was ridiculous. She had a sudden mental image of Simon, in green designer wellies, turning the earth with a stainless-steel spade while the naked body of a murdered girl glinted white in the moonlight.

Simon said warily, 'When did amalgam fillings come in exactly?'

'1886, sir. I don't think you need be worried – though they are still in use today among National Health patients.' Sarah watched the Inspector deciding whether to offer another tit-bit of information. She supposed he had to play with people, teasing out what he knew to observe their reactions. 'We've had to do a radioactive assay on those bones. Very tedious and expensive. What with the cutbacks, anything like that these days has to be justified. What it tells us – the assay – what it tells us . . . .' If he had a pipe, he'd be filling it, tamping down tobacco and watching from under lowered eyelids to see whether Simon and Sarah had begun to sweat. The man was a sadist, no doubt of that: Sarah wouldn't care to be on the wrong end of any interrogation *he* might be conducting. She remembered her school friend, Marilyn, kicked and thumped in the police van after what was, practically speaking, a non-violent demonstration against polluted water. 'What the assay tells us is that there were no radioisotopes in the bones. Consequently she died before atmospheric nuclear testing began. Then the dentist says – very helpful fellow, the dentist – that bone loss in the jaw indicates the probability of Vincent's Disease, which was common among young adults during the war years. And we are left with . . .' – the man was grinning at them like some bloody uncle or a game-show host announcing a popular win – 'We are left with a year of death probably in the late nineteen-forties and certainly not after, unless the young lady spent most of her life in Antarctica. Before your time, anyway.'

'So what are you going to do?'

'Pursue our enquiries, Mrs Arnott. Open a file.'

'She'd have had to be a stranger to the village.'

'Why?'

'If anyone from a local family had disappeared, it would have been known. Reported. There'd be a record.'

'Right!' He had become a kindly schoolteacher, encouraging her to think on. Simon shifted uneasily in his chair.

'Late nineteen-forties, you said? Wasn't there an old tramp murdered at . . . somewhere over near . . . one of the villages? I've read about it. Some sort of ritual murder.'

'They stuck a pitchfork through him and hung him up like a scarecrow to bleed over the crops. Before my time. Never solved. But that was reported, the day after it happened, by the driver of the school bus. It's hardly comparable with the present case.'

'Nobody would talk? Frightened?'

'Right! In our case, fear's not the problem; it's forgetfulness. Most people concerned are very likely dead, and the rest won't be able to remember – or say they can't. It's bound to be a low-scale kind of a thing, given police resources as they are, but a murder file is never closed.'

'You said it wasn't murder.'

'No, I don't think I said that, did I? I said there were no signs of any violent cause of death, which is not quite the same thing.'

Simon said, 'Do you mean to tell me that every one of us alive today has radioisotopes in his bones because of nuclear testing?'

During the night, the young woman came to her, dressed in mid-seventeenth century costume, the costume of the Civil War. Her dark hair was decently covered with a white bonnet, and her long dress was of a soft gray like the breast of a pigeon, with the bodice cut low and long full sleeves. She stretched out her arms to Sarah, then withdrew them slowly when they became filled with the baby she held to her breast.

Sarah took Jonathan from the young woman and returned him to his cot. She said, 'You've got it all wrong. It was the late nineteen-forties. There's an amalgam filling in one of your teeth.'

The young woman did not reply, but stood there at the end of the bed gazing at Sarah, clearly wanting something but unable to say what it was, being prevented by the deep wound in her throat, which had been slit from ear to ear, a fate she had passively endured.

Simon spoke from inside Sarah's head, a space he did not usually occupy, it being reserved for Sarah's mother and the homeopathic therapist. He said, 'I don't think throats ever are slit from ear to ear, are they? It's Jack the Ripper stuff, that kind of thing. Penny Dreadfuls. You'd find the Adam's apple got in the way.'

What did Simon know about Penny Dreadfuls? He was

one of the computer generation: he had never read a book, whereas Sarah had always been old for her years.

The ha-ha and the rockery had been completed. Jeremy and Clyde had moved on and out of the garden, except that Sarah could not be expected to do the watering and the weeding, the spraying and pruning, the hoeing, manuring and mulching all by herself, and Simon had no taste for it, so the Arnotts had taken out a maintenance contract. Until a man could be found from the village, the garden would receive professional attention from Jeremy Potter, Personalised Garden Design, one afternoon a week. Since there was unemployment in the village, one would have thought that a man might be easy to find, but the village men were not gardeners these days nor did their wives do cleaning: Sarah was paying five pounds an hour, a tradesman's wage, to Elsie, her cleaning lady, who had worked in the ticket office of the railway station at Hockley Heath until British Rail had made her redundant. The principle of equal pay for women and the decline in government subsidy had between them done for Elsie.

In the Arnotts' weekending days the garden had been as basic as the furnishings of the house, with a lawn, a few shrubs, annuals bought annually from a garden centre, a clematis and a Virginia creeper against one wall which, receiving no care, died in a hard winter to be replaced in the spring. Only the conservatory, bought from a catalogue which came unsolicited in the post, might have been considered as going it a bit, but even that, though fanciful in its design, had been basic in use, with canvas chairs for sitting out and a few pelargoniums in pots. Now the garden had height and status, reflecting Simon's own position as Promotions Manager, directly responsible to the Board. The shrubs had become a shrubbery, there were alpines in the rock garden, marsh marigold and mimulus in the water garden; cordon apples had been planted against a wooden fence, a fig (which would not fruit for several years) in the conservatory, and Simon talked of starting an asparagus bed. Sarah looked at all this work, but did not see that it was good. She and Simon had not done it; Jeremy had done it. Simon would say they never could have done it, not by themselves, not being garden people really, but Sarah would have liked to have a go – slowly, bit by bit, learning from her mistakes. They didn't need a ha-ha. What did it matter if the cattle ate the shrubs?

She supposed that the police must be pursuing their enquiries in the village. There would still be villagers who had been alive in the late 1940s, the murderer perhaps amongst them. 1949, say – people in their mid-twenties then would be in their mid-sixties now. Of course, 'late nineteen-forties' was only a guess. Whatever Vincent's Disease was, it must have been about before the war years as well as during; if it was a disease of malnutrition, it would have been rife among working-class people all through the 1920s and 1930s. She went to find *The Guide To Family Health*, and looked up Vincent's Disease, discovering that it had nothing to do with malnutrition but was brought about by smoking. Women – working-class women – would have smoked particularly heavily during the war years. Late 1940s, then. She reminded herself that there was no proof of murder: it might only be concealment of death. And why should she assume that the woman was working-class?

There was a heatwave. It had been made official. Temperatures in Towcester were higher than in Tenerife. Jonathan grew fractious. This was a source of some distress to Sarah, who no longer knew if he were hungry or simply hot. There was also the possibility that he might be teething: the books seemed to disagree about when this might happen: four months, though early, could not be ruled out. She tried rubbing his gums with a finger. They were certainly hard, but was there a small pale bump which would indicate a tooth? Jonathan seemed disposed to treat her finger as an auxiliary nipple, which was not, as Sarah told him severely, the name of the game. Perhaps she herself should make some enquiries in the village about the murdered girl. She could ask at the butcher's – start from there anyway: it seemed appropriate.

She would have to take Jonathan with her. That was it about a baby, often delightfully it, sometimes inconveniently it: he could never be left behind. Simon had spoken about an au pair, and maybe it would come to that, but not yet. If the young woman had smoked heavily, to the point of contracting Vincent's Disease, it would have affected the foetus. The young women of the late 1940s didn't know about the dangers of smoking during pregnancy or they would not have done it. Sarah herself did sometimes smoke a cigarette of an evening nowadays if she and Simon were doing something stressful like entertaining visitors, but she never bought them: she cadged them from the guests. And anyway, since moving to the country, they hardly ever did entertain.

Things changed so quickly. Between the discovery of the skeleton and the Detective Inspector's visit, her milk had begun to go. The books said it would not go, but would continue to be produced to match the baby's appetite. Perhaps Jonathan's appetite was inordinate. He was given the breast now only at morning and evening, with frequent bottles during the day. Jonathan had ambitions towards self-sufficiency, gratifying but also a little disturbing to a mother: he preferred to hold the bottle for himself with both hands, though he had not so far managed to raise it high enough to drink without assistance. Sarah had begun to try him with mashed banana, but he treated it as old men in hospital treat unwelcome medicines, concealing it in the pockets of his cheeks to be extruded later. Any baby had a right to be fractious when one considered the difficulties of communication with adults.

Six o'clock! There was some kind of crisis in Promotions. Simon had taken to getting home later than Drinks' Time, and dinner had become a moveable feast. He did not seem to feel deprived at seeing so little of his son. Sometimes, sitting at table or in the conservatory with Jonathan rocking in his canvas chair between them, she had noticed that, when she turned away, as any mother might, to retrieve a plastic rabbit, suck its ears and put it back in her son's mouth, and Simon happened to be in the middle of a sentence, he would often look quite cross and the sentence would trail away, to be followed by a silence.

She picked Jonathan up, fractious as he was, and crooned to him. 'Baa, baa, black sheep! Have you any wool? Yes, sir; yes, sir, three bags full.' It was odd that one still calmed one's children with nursery rhymes; everyone did, still did, old songs passed down, Sarah supposed, unconsciously from generation to generation, never the Top Ten. Why did Sarah not pull songs out of her own youth? Fifteen years ago, when she was herself fifteen, there had been a group called the Bay City Rollers. She remembered them still; they were Scottish; they had worn football scarves, and been extremely highly esteemed by Sarah and her friends. Yet she could not now remember even one of their Greatest Hits. She had a sudden memory of her mother, assembling a *daube* in the pine kitchen at home and, believing herself unobserved, singing *Groovy Kind of Love*, an all-time great by the Mindbenders. Sarah's mother had known all the words. She would. The hell with her! '*Frère Jacques, frère Jacques*,' Sarah sang to her fractious son, jiggling him against her breast, '*Dormez-vous, dormez-vous? Sonnez les matinées, sonnez les matinées. Din, din, don! Din, din, don!*'

She left Jonathan in the car outside the butcher's, strapped into his baby seat with the front windows down so that the customers could coo at him as they went in and out. Sarah enjoyed shopping in the village, because she could do it a bit at a time with conversation, whereas the superstore outside Leamington, although cheaper and with its own parking and with aisles wide enough for two baby carriages to pass abreast, was so absurdly well-stocked that it almost enjoined one to buy in bulk and spend the next four days at home. Sarah was not lonely, and could be well content with her own company and that of her son, but she did like to get out of the house occasionally.

Rob Barton, the butcher, was on his own that morning, and only old Mrs Potter, Jeremy's grandmother, was in the shop, buying mince. Bartons, Garbetts and Dasts were the old village families: the Potters were newcomers, having arrived in 1923. 'How are you getting on with that skeleton of yours?' Rob said. The village people liked a subject to last.

'There's going to be an inquest.'

'What, on that? Civil War rubbish!'

'Don't make no difference. Coroner's got to sit on it. That's the law,' old Mrs Potter said. 'What have you got in this mince besides fat and gristle?'

'Human remains.'

'I believe you.'

So they all had a good laugh. Old Mrs Potter would repeat Rob's witticism and her capping of it in the Spar later. Sarah said, 'How old were you in the late forties, Rob? 1949, say.'

'Two. Baby boom, I was. 1947. Ten new babies in the village that year, never been matched. Men came back from the war. Full employment then, not like now. Bright future – bang! bang! they went at it.'

Sarah remembered the eight-month foetus, its bones still neatly curled inside its mother. 'Baby boom. Yes,' she said. 'There was, of course. I came later. 1960.'

'Still a good time, the sixties. Six-a-side football. All gone now. They haven't got the interest.'

'Is there anyone who could tell me what the village was like then?'

Rob indicated Mrs Potter. 'Horse's mouth,' he said.

'Of course. Stupid of me.'

'Plenty of us,' Mrs Potter said. 'We don't move out, you know, not the older people. The younger people move – they have to: there's no work – or they improve themselves. Bobby Dast went to Australia. Canada – there's some gone to Canada. Some go nursing, some married out of the village, some down to London . . . Oxford . . . Maidstone: Jimmy Garbett's in Basingstoke; he's in the insurance, doing ever so well. There's no homes for the young ones, even if they wanted to stay.'

Mrs Potter would not be getting at Sarah. A barn conversion is not a starter home: the Arnotts had not deprived any younger villagers of the opportunity to settle near their parents. Jeremy's own house had been purpose-built, a present from his father, and contained a jacuzzi. Sarah said, 'I suppose you can remember everyone who was in the village then?'

'If I put myself to it.'

How did one ask the question? If Rob could still talk about 'Civil War rubbish', the information given by the Detective Inspector to the Arnotts was not yet general knowledge. There had been nothing about it in the local paper, though Sarah supposed it would all come out at the inquest, whenever that was. Sarah did things on impulse; that was her trouble, as her mother had frequently pointed out. She had decided to ask at the butcher's without knowing exactly what her question would be. 'Was there a village girl who disappeared suddenly back in 1948 or 49?' – they would know at once that the skeleton had been dated: why else would Sarah be asking? Why hadn't the police themselves been asking the question about the village? There must be a reason, and if Sarah asked when the police had not, she would be in trouble. Both Rob and old Mrs Potter were looking at her; she would have to come up with something. 'I've been wondering,' she said. 'I've got so much time on my hands these days.' (Lies! lies! she had no time at all. Jonathan took up all her time.) 'I've been thinking of starting a sort of local history project. For the Open University, maybe. I haven't really decided yet.'

'Oh, a project!' Rob knew about projects. The children did them at school. 'What's it going to be about, then?'

'I thought I'd do a sort of Domesday Book – then and now – except that it would be people not property. List all the people of the village in the late forties – 1948, say – and follow up their lives to find out what happened to them – who prospered and who . . . .' One couldn't say 'failed'. '. . . and who didn't. Who went to Canada and Australia, as Mrs Potter said, or found jobs and settled down elsewhere in England, and who stayed. Not just the old village families, of course, but everyone, strangers as well – people who came in to do a particular job, and left when they'd done it. It's fascinating what one might find out. Maybe some people just disappeared altogether, no knowing what happened to them.'

She had been improvising, and had gone over the top. Such a project would take months – years. And perhaps that bit about the people who had totally disappeared was a bit too close. Never mind! 'Strangers?' old Mrs Potter said.

'They'd be the difficult ones. I'd be so grateful if you could help me.'

'No good asking me. I can't remember that far back, I'm sure. 1948! Funny year to choose, neither one thing nor the other.' And she left the shop with her mince.

A promising source seemed suddenly to have dried up. Sarah said, 'Did I say something to offend her? I'm sorry if I did.'

Rob said, 'Don't you worry; that's just her way – bit abrupt sometimes. Known for it.'

The inquest was adjourned, as it was bound to be when nobody knew the identity of the corpse, and the police were still pursuing their enquiries. Sarah meanwhile pursued her own enquiries, but met with no success. There is a limit to what can be said while shopping, and a limit to the amount of shopping one can do for two adults and a baby. She considered knocking on doors, but what would one say? 'Excuse me. I'm looking for a young woman who disappeared from around these parts in the late forties.' Village women were said to dislike taking strangers into their homes. It would all have to be done on the doorstep.

She asked Simon if he would go down to the pub one evening and engage the older regulars in conversation, but he refused. 'It'd be out of character. I don't go to pubs.'

'They wouldn't know that. You could go this once.'

'Why can't you go with me?'

'Jonathan.'

'Take him with us. We can leave him in the car.'

'We'd have to stay in the Saloon Bar. They don't like women in the Public Bar, which is where all the regulars go.'

'What a lot you seem to know about village life!'

'I get it from books.'

'Some of it may be out of date. We have been into that pub, if you remember, that Sunday the papers weren't delivered. Scampi in the basket, horse brasses and fruit machines! I don't think they had a downmarket bit for the regulars.'

'You'll go, then?'

'I'd feel silly. I don't know why you're so bothered. She's nothing to do with us.'

'I dream about her.'

But he wouldn't go. He couldn't see himself doing it. Simon was as unsure of himself as she was, in his own way: being above concern was part of the unsureness. That was why they had married, she supposed, like turning to like. 'The point is,' she said to Jonathan, 'I was never really good at anything. People go on about making a life of one's own, but what would I have done? I might as well have married as not, and at least it's meant I've got you.' She didn't, of course, mean that 'people' went on about it: she meant her mother, but Jonathan knew that.

The weather continued warm. Sarah drove down to the village and walked Jonathan in his pushchair. In this way she would be able to converse naturally over garden walls with women of the right age who might happen to be weeding or dead-heading their roses. She would begin by admiring their gardens, then turn the conversation to her own and so to the skeleton which had been unearthed in it – she had decided to abandon the cover story about the Open University, which was clearly going to be too complicated to keep afloat.

The plan was easier to conceive than to carry out. The village women seldom weeded at the right conversational distance from the road. Sarah's opening remark had to be made in a louder voice than is usual in casual encounters. 'What?' the women would say, 'Did you want something?' and come running, after which a natural conversation became impossible and the switch from the beauties of their own gardens to the skeleton discovered at Garbett's Barn seemed somehow accusatory. The manner of the village women became abrupt and they would move towards the house when they saw Mrs Arnott and her baby approaching.

A car stopped beside Sarah. The Detective Inspector was driving. It was not a police car, and must be his own, a Volvo, quite an expensive model, with electrically operated windows, one of which he now lowered to speak to her.

'How are you doing?'

'Sorry?' She had to bend over to talk to him. It put her immediately at a disadvantage.

'I heard you'd been asking about.'

'I'm interested.'

'An interested party? What's the nature of your interest?'

Why did the man have to turn everything the wrong way? Sarah said, 'She was found on our land. We have a right to know who she is, and she has a right to be known.'

'Could you be asking the wrong question?'

'Sorry?'

'Don't ask who disappeared. Nobody disappeared – not as far as anyone around here knows – or, as you yourself said, there'd be a record of it. Ask who was pregnant.'

Sarah saw at once that he was right. She said, 'I can't talk to you, bent over like this.'

He switched the engine off and got out, but kept the car between them. Sarah said, 'If you know the right question, why can't you ask it yourself?'

'Been doing. Got nowhere – just like you. Interesting! You'd think the doctors would help. Should be on somebody's list – ante-natal stuff – orange juice and rose-hip syrup as it was then. But there's been so much buggering around with the National Health Service. Two practices have gone out of existence, and the new lot's only been here three years. Anyway, we can't know she was from this village. Could be any of the villages around here. Could be Leamington. Bit of an extended investigation in that case. There were a lot of pregnancies in Leamington at the end of the nineteen-forties. Baby boom! And they had the Free Czech Army there; that pushed up the average.'

Sarah said, 'I've already heard about the baby boom.'

'Tell you what, why don't you have a word with Miss Hedges in the Nursing Home at Glazeby? Used to be the schoolteacher here. She's in her eighties now. People that age can't remember what happened five minutes ago, but you ask them about the old days and there's no stopping them.'

'Why don't your people ask her?'

'Old lady. Doesn't do to have the police asking questions. Bound to upset her. And it affects the Home too. Police come calling, people gossip – nasty taste. But you'd just be a visitor. Old people in homes like getting visitors, hunger for them, to tell you the truth; it's a matter of status. They don't get many – children forget, you see, and anyway Miss Hedges never had any kids. You'd give her pleasure. I approve of that. Don't get many opportunities for giving pleasure myself.'

Sarah said, 'But somebody did disappear.'

'No. Somebody went away. Somebody who was expected to leave the village left as expected. Or else was never here in the first place. And anyone who knows different isn't saying. I dare say you'll let me know if you find anything.'

And he climbed back into the car, started the engine, and drove away. Sarah discovered that both the women in the two nearest gardens had moved well within conversational distance, but she took no advantage of it and returned to her own car instead.

The staff were getting Miss Hedges up, so Sarah waited in the hall. The time was just past eleven of a fine summer morning, which seemed late as an hour for rising, even for a lady in her eighties, but, if each of the thirty-six residents required assistance, and the staff were few, the process of getting up would, Sarah supposed, have to be stretched over several hours and perhaps Miss Hedges was a long way down the queue. Would going to bed present the same problems? Clearly it would. Going to bed would have to begin just after tea, and, on the same system, the first up would be the first away. And what did they find to do in between?

She could see what they did; they sat in the Common Room. The door between it and the hall stood open, and Sarah could see inside. The furniture was oddly arranged, with armchairs against all four walls, even the window walls, and no furniture in the centre of the room at all, just a ginger cat curled up on the carpet. The armchairs by the windows faced half outwards, all the others inwards, so that a few of the residents had a view of the outside world, the rest only a view of each other, except that this morning those facing the door could also see Sarah standing about in the hall.

She had come alone. If you had asked her why, she would have explained that she did not wish to risk Jonathan's making a disturbance (not that he ever did) and upsetting the old people, so she had left him at home with Elsie, it being Elsie's day. In fact it was Jonathan whom she did not wish to upset. He had no experience of old people. Sarah's mother was not old – fifty-eight is certainly not old – and his great-grandparents on both sides were dead. Sarah's intention was that Jonathan would never grow old: she would protect him from that as from every other unpleasantness. By the time Jonathan was eighty, something would have been invented against old age.

The chairs inside the Common Room had been pushed close together and Sarah counted eight of the old ladies within who could see through the open door. They did not speak, they hardly seemed to blink, but watched her steadily. Only their toothless mouths moved in a perpetual chewing motion. It was really very uncomfortable being watched by eight unblinking old ladies. A middle-aged woman in uniform came from the kitchen area to the office by the front door. She had an air of authority, considerably more so than the plump nurse to whom Sarah had given her name on arrival. Sarah said, 'Excuse me! Will Miss Hedges be long?'

'You're her visitor, aren't you? Getting her up takes as long as it takes, I'm afraid. Depends if she's feeling obstreperous.'

'Is she often obstreperous?'

'Miss Hedges? Only verbally, not like some. She shouldn't be long. Would you like somewhere to sit?' She looked through the door at the unblinking ladies. 'You're entertainment at the moment, but if you get too restive you might be construed as a threat.'

'Couldn't you shut the door?'

'They hate that. You can wait in the Library.'

Sarah imagined somewhere filled with large-print books, with perhaps a few writing pads and letter-racks and magnifying glasses on chains. In fact there were only three books in the Library and no writing materials at all. The room seemed to double as the Staff Dining Room, and was almost filled by a round table, its top much marked by hot dishes. There were also four dining chairs and a bookcase which, besides the three books stacked horizontally on the bottom shelf, contained old copies of the *Readers' Digest* and *Women's World*, seven jigsaw puzzles and a board and counters for snakes and ladders. Sarah picked up the top book to see what the unblinking old ladies were given to read. It was called *Great Escape Stories*.

The smell of cabbage came in gusts from the kitchen next door, and steel cutlery fell or was thrown about on trays of melamine. After some time, a young nurse in jeans and a T-shirt, with shoulder-length hair and a Viva Zapata moustache, wheeled Miss Hedges to the Library. 'I'm not sure I can get the wheelchair through the door,' he said. 'Would you like to take her outside? It's quite warm, and I brought her cardie.'

Miss Hedges said to the nurse, 'Who is she? I don't know her.'

'Forgotten you, I expect,' the nurse said to Sarah. 'Don't let it worry you.'

'I have not forgotten her. I never knew her. She's a stranger to me.'

'She's your visitor.'

Sarah said, 'I'm Sarah Arnott. I live on the hill above Radcote.'

Miss Hedges said to the nurse, 'Jehovah's Witness. She's wasting her time. Wheel me back.'

'I'd like to ask you some questions. About the village in the old days.'

'Make your mind up,' the nurse said to Miss Hedges. 'I haven't got all day. There's plenty of the other girls would enjoy a visitor if you're going to be haughty,' and to Sarah, 'mind you put the brake on. We've had more than one of our old ladies spill into the shrubbery.'

At the top of the lawn, there was a bench under a monkey-puzzle tree. Sarah, who was unused to managing a wheelchair on grass and had made heavy weather of the slope, was glad to position the chair in a patch of shade, set the brake and sit down. Miss Hedges looked across the valley with satisfaction. The Nursing Home at Glazeby was at the edge of the village, with a clear view from the grounds of pasture running down to a small river, now almost dry, a water meadow beyond, then fields of ripe barley and of beans, farm buildings, trees, a road. 'I enjoy diversity,' she said. 'We don't get much indoors,' and breathed deeply several times, in and out, as if warming up for a PE class. 'Have you seen the Common Room?'

'I looked in.'

'Bedlam. Hogarth – *Rake's Progress*. And I was quite the opposite, you know – clean-living . . . prudish really. Hardly seems worthwhile. None of the fun, and it all comes down to the same thing in the end. The old are children, and our own children control us.'

'But you have no children.'

'Nephew. I never see him.'

'How did you get in here?'

'Arthritis. Needed a hip replacement. Non-urgent surgery – National Health – wait seven years. Meanwhile I fell downstairs and broke the hip, along with several other bits and pieces. Helpless. Couldn't look after myself, and there was nobody to look after me – wham! in here! – paperwork done in a day. They sold my cottage, and that paid the fees for a while. Better dead, of course, but they don't allow that.'

'Is there nobody you can talk to? No companionship?'

'You saw them.' Miss Hedges shook her head, and snorted like a bull terrier, but in self-reproof. 'Damn! Uncharitable! Black mark, that girl! Still . . . fact remains . . . odd one out. Not many of them are cripples . . . not many old maids, eh? Grandmothers, great-grandmothers – the reason most of them get sent here is senility. Not called that, of course. "Loss of short-term memory" sounds better – suggests you've mislaid it and might get it back, but nobody does. Leave the gas on . . . electric fires . . . water running . . . danger to themselves and others . . . kindness really to put them somewhere they'll be properly looked after. The married daughters come to see them for a while, bring the kids . . . does no good. They get worse, you see. No stimulus: they rot. Half-blind – they can't read – if they ever did. Deaf – you can't hold a conversation. Bloody awful company, to tell you the truth. Talk to myself most of the time. And Adrian and I have a bit of a rabbit sometimes, if he's nothing much else to do – he's the one who brought me down. But he won't stay. None of the staff stays for long. What do you want to know about the village?'

'*Can't remember what happened five minutes ago.*' Sarah

began to feel an anger against the Inspector. 'There was a man told me your own short-term memory wasn't very good.'

'Policeman? CID? He's been here. I wouldn't talk to him. Sent you, did he?'

'Suggested I should come. Why wouldn't you talk to him?'

'One of my scratchy days. And I don't like the police.' Another snort. 'Ask your questions.'

'You were teaching at the school just after the war?'

'And during. And since. Forty years. I retired in seventy-two, but I stayed on in the village, as I expect you've been told.'

'I'm thinking about nineteen forty-nine – maybe forty-eight, maybe fifty.' It seemed rather a silly question to Sarah now that she had to come out with it. 'Do you remember which of the village women were pregnant?'

'Lots.'

'A young woman between eighteen and twenty-five.'

'Unmarried, do you mean?'

'I'm not sure. Probably.'

'Why do you want to know?'

There being no reason for concealment, Sarah told her. Miss Hedges listened carefully, doing her breathing exercises and snorting from time to time, and when Sarah had finished, she closed her eyes and fell silent. Sarah waited. Miss Hedges opened her eyes again, and said, 'That's what I used to tell the children. Always count to five before answering. What do you feel about war crimes?'

'Sorry?'

'Old men – my age or thereabouts – dragged out of comfortable obscurity in Pittsburgh or Paraguay – or even Glasgow, I believe, though I can't think why anyone should want to retire to Glasgow – and prosecuted for something that happened over fifty years ago. You approve of that?'

'It's not the same.'

'Isn't it? I think it is. "Vengeance is *mine*," saith the Lord. "*I* shall repay." There's no evidence that He does, of course. The wicked shall flourish like the green bay tree. They all became dentists. I suppose that was a natural progression from running a concentration camp.'

'You're making fun of me.'

'No. Trying to get you to see what you're at.'

'I dream about her.'

'We dream about ourselves, Sarah Arnott.'

'She has a right – I think she has a right. To be known. To have it known how and why she died.'

'The dead have no rights. Wheel me in.'

For a moment Sarah contemplated refusing. They would sit there until Miss Hedges cracked, or else Adrian would come to her. Sarah released the brake of the wheelchair and said, 'You know who she was, then?' Miss Hedges snorted again. Sarah said, 'She has a right to peace.'

'Romantic flummery! Codswallop! I've no time for it. She's dead: that's her peace. You've seen the bones.'

'I've seen the bones of her baby inside her, Miss Hedges. You never had any children.'

'Hundreds. And loved most of them. Forty years, remember. Children and their children; they all came to me.' They had reached the path. 'Wait!' Sarah waited. 'Brake!' She set the brake. 'I had an assistant from nineteen forty-six to forty-eight. Temporary staff on supply; you had to take what you could get in those days – still do. Doris Reeves. No need to write it down. Reeves, like the watercolours: you'll remember that. Dorrie! We weren't close, but we rubbed along well enough. She wasn't a local girl, lodged at the vicarage. Mother lived in Nottingham. Father ran back to the East six months after demobilisation, and married a rubber planter's daughter – bigamously, I imagine, since the mother wouldn't divorce him. Ungenerous woman. Dorrie didn't care for her much, but she went home to mother to have her baby. Never saw her again.'

'Didn't it cause talk in the village, the teacher not coming back?'

'Why should it? End of term. She was only supply staff. Going to have a baby. Nobody expected her back.'

'Who was the father?'

'Wouldn't say.'

'But everyone knew?'

'Nobody knew.'

'Did she write to you from Nottingham?'

'Why should she?'

'I would have.'

'Packed all her stuff. Went off with it. She had a car – secondhand Morris Eight, bought it for twopence. Sold it to the vicar's wife before she left. I always thought that odd.' There was the sound of a bell from indoors. 'Lunch! Brake off! You don't want Adrian flapping; he feels betrayed very easily. Will you come and see me again?'

'I'll try.'

'But you'll fail. Don't blame you. I never cared for the old when I was your age – still don't, as a matter of fact.'

They were back inside the building, and Adrian's moustache twitched at Sarah reproachfully as he carried trays into the Common Room. Each tray was fitted with arms which locked into position on the arms of the chairs, confining the occupants behind a barrier of mashed potatoes and frozen peas. Sarah said, 'Is there anything you'd like me to bring? Anything you want?'

'Books. Always want books. Anything literate. Anything you've read yourself, and don't want to keep. Detective stories. Pornography. Thackeray, if you have any, but no Gissing, no Mrs Gaskell and none of that magical realism rubbish. Thank you for coming. I enjoyed the visit.'

TO THE NORTH

'*We dream about ourselves, Sarah Arnott.*' It was not true. Sarah's skeleton had not been found at the bottom of the garden. Her son, Jonathan, did not lie dead in her womb, but had emerged very much alive and been admired by all present at the occasion, including his father.

Who had been murdered, Doris Reeves or she who had once been Sarah Bridges and was now Sarah Arnott? Yes, it might be said, in the language of dreams, that Sarah Bridges was dead, the possible potential Sarah Bridges for whom her mother had hoped God knows what, but Sarah Arnott was alive and actual. It might be said, in the language of dreams, that Sarah Arnott had murdered Sarah Bridges, but what of that? Sarah Bridges had been nobody in particular. Sarah Arnott had a role and function; she was a wife and mother.

A role and a function. If there's nothing you particularly want to do in life and not much you're good at, marriage gives you a role and a function, and that is enormously strengthened when you have a child. But it ties you to one particular person, and that person to you.

Luckily she had no objection to being tied to Simon, no great objection, and not for most of the time. She had chosen to tie herself to Simon; it had been a free choice, unconstrained and responsible; she had known him for long enough, known exactly what she was taking on, had already grown used to him through eighteen months of weekend and holiday cohabitation, and a further six in the Fulham flat.

'*We dream about ourselves.*' In Sarah's case, what had been murdered (in the language of dreams) was not a person, but merely an illusion about the potentiality of Sarah Bridges, an illusion entertained not by Sarah herself, but by her mother. There had, in or out of the language of dreams, been no murder, none, just a rational decision to accept reality. Sarah decided that she would not go and see Miss Hedges again too soon; it would be arousing expectations she could not hope to fulfil. She made up a parcel of books to send instead.

What Miss Hedges had said about war crimes lodged in her mind. She decided not to tell the Inspector about the Morris Eight which had been bought by the vicar's wife. She would tell him about Doris Reeves, the assistant at the village school, pregnant by some person unknown, who had gone back to her mother in Nottingham to have the baby and had never been heard from again, because nobody had expected to hear from her. That should be enough; the police ought to be able to make an identification from that. Sarah was not paid to do the work of the police for them.

She decided that – simply for the interest, and for no other reason – she would try to find out what had happened to the vicar's wife. Miss Hedges was right. If one were already eight months pregnant, and with a lot of gear to carry, one wouldn't sell one's Morris Eight to the vicar's wife, but use it to get back to Nottingham.

'*We dream about ourselves.*' It had never been possible for Sarah to explain to her mother why she had married Simon. If she had been forced into a truthful answer, which of course she never was, she might have said, 'The emptiness'. She supposed that it would be as difficult for Simon to explain to his own mother why he had married Sarah, except that Simon's mother would not ask the question, seeming to believe that, within reasonable limits, one wife was as good as another.

Because of Jonathan, Sarah's life was no longer empty, but she did often feel unfulfilled.

For a time she did nothing – or nothing in particular: she sent the parcel of books off to Miss Hedges with a little note to say she had very much enjoyed the visit, and hoped to come again at some future date. She did nothing to get in touch with the Detective Inspector, because she could be reasonably sure that he would get in touch with her, and so he did, telephoning on a Tuesday morning, with the dishes still to be washed and a bucket full of nappies, full to overflowing as a matter of fact, not that this disconcerted Sarah greatly, since she had become used to the fact that, with a baby not yet six months old, housework accumulates faster than one can ever hope to get on top of it. Sarah disapproved of disposable nappies on environmental grounds.

'How did it go with Miss Hedges?'

'I've been to see her. We had a long talk. She's very lively – very bright. She shouldn't be in there.' Sarah knew that this was hardly the Inspector's fault, but wished to blame somebody since she was already feeling guilty about the little note.

'Did you talk about our friend?'

'A bit.'

'And?'

'She gave me a name.'

'I'll come round.'

'There's not that much to tell. I could give you all the information over the phone.'

'I'll come round anyway.'

He arrived at lunchtime. Sarah made a quiche. The CID, it had begun to seem to her, took food and drink for granted.

'Nottingham,' he said. 'It's a pretty little problem. She'd had very little dental work done, but I suppose there might be enough to risk an identification.'

Sarah said, 'I don't see how you could. It's nearly fifty years ago. The dentist would be dead, and the practice mightn't exist any more. Anyway, there could be more than one – a school dentist, and then someone else when she was grown up – maybe somewhere far from Nottingham, when she was at Teacher Training College.' She had been to the village shop and bought lager, and now the man was drinking spritzers again; he had clearly developed a taste for them, and she and Simon, she supposed, were responsible.

'You may be right.'

'Means you don't think so.'

'Dentists do die: practices are sold. But what do you buy when you buy a practice, Mrs Arnott? You buy the patients, which means you buy the records. Useful people, dentists: I've always had time for them. There'd have been a mouth chart made at her first visit, and if she'd gone to somebody else later, the new man would have made another. Then, as long as she was NHS – which she almost certainly was – there's the Dental Estimates Board in Eastbourne, with records going back to the beginning of the Health Service. Now we've got a name and we've got a jaw with a full set of teeth, and, if they match, we can match them.'

'And then?'

'Then we know she never did leave the village, that she died between announcing her intention to leave and actually doing so. And we work backwards.'

'You mean you've begun to take it seriously?'

'We always take murder seriously. It's not a matter of

seriousness: it's a matter of urgency – what we call the language of priorities. When you begin to have some chance of clearing a crime up, it becomes more urgent. Not yet overpoweringly so in this case, if I may say so, but worth pursuing for a while anyway. She was eight months pregnant. Next step, find the father.'

'Miss Hedges said nobody knew who he was.'

'Somebody always knows. He knew, for a start, unless it was a one-night stand. Now, go back eight months. She left – was thought to have left – believed to have gone back home to have the baby – at the end of a school term. No, I tell a lie. They weren't expecting her back. Therefore, probably at the end of the school year, though your Miss Hedges didn't say so.' Already Miss Hedges had become Sarah's by virtue of one visit. 'Easy to find out. Question is, where was she eight months before when the baby was conceived – in the village or in Nottingham? School year ends in June. Eight months earlier, October/November. She was in the village, working as assistant to Miss Hedges. And if she was seeing any of the village lads . . . young men . . . older men . . . married men on a regular basis, most of the village knew about it, including Miss Hedges.'

'I'm not going back to cross-examine her.'

'Nor am I. Counterproductive. We can ask about. Start with the parish register, and make a list of possible men – which, practically speaking, means all the men between the age of puberty and obsolescence.'

'"We" can ask about?'

'Not you.'

'No!' Sarah had no intention of asking about in that area. She had already offended old Mrs Potter by asking questions far less personal. Yet it was odd that the Inspector should be so strongly against her continuing to ask about, when so far he had found it useful. 'Why not?'

'Could be dangerous.'

She stared at him. The idea was lunatic. Any man who

might be the father of Dorrie Reeves's baby had to be in his sixties, if he were not already dead. What danger could an old-age pensioner represent? Was she to be battered to death with a walking frame or smothered with a truss?

'Village people don't like strangers poking about in their private affairs. I'm a stranger too, of course, but I'm the police; it's my job. They'll just clam up with me. Maybe I'll be able to winkle something out of the silence, maybe not. Maybe there'll be someone glad of the chance to settle an old score – anonymously, of course. I'll see how I go. But if you start asking about, then even the ones who know bugger-all will resent it – pardon my French. They'll resent anything from an outsider. You'd be unpopular at best.'

'And at worst?'

'You're very isolated out here.'

'Half the village are outsiders. Yuppies like us. Midland Yuppies: they commute to Solihull.'

'That's the half you need'nt be afraid of. With the old villagers it's different – partly *because* of the Yuppies. The resentment's always there, you see; it only needs an excuse to come out. I think you know that's true, Mrs Arnott.'

'So . . . no more questions? From me?'

'Right. It's just routine police work from now on, working our way through the parish register. Which of the men are still around? Who's gone away and where did he go? Then question them – and their wives . . . brothers . . . sisters: I expect the whole village is related.' He was on his second piece of quiche, and enjoying it. 'And it may all be wasted. We don't know the father was from the village. Could have been a regular boyfriend, come over from Nottingham or wherever for the weekend. Could have been from another village, could have been from Leamington.'

'The Free Czech Army.'

'They'd all gone home by 1946, though some of them came back after 1948. You might say the Free Czech Army are the only people who are positively in the clear.' He wiped his mouth with the back of his sleeve, and seemed about to go.

'You'll let me know how you get on?'

'No need for that, Mrs Arnott. You'll hear if anybody's arrested. Better for you to keep out of it from now on. There's some resentment already, you know, about your activities. Just a bit of feeling. No reason to blow it up further.'

Sarah was glad she had kept quiet about the Morris Eight. Having used her to get at Miss Hedges, the Inspector clearly regarded her as dispensable. She was not to be a partner in his investigation, not even a sounding-board; she supposed he would have a Sergeant for that like Inspector Morse, since he clearly did enjoy sounding off, enjoyed the attention. He would go elsewhere for his quiche and spritzers, elsewhere (if he should need it) for unpaid amateur assistance. Allowed to hang about, she was liable to clog the smooth running of the police machinery.

And he could not even come right out and say as much; she might have accepted it if he had. No, it must all seem to be done out of concern for her; she must be protected from the revenges of resentful yokels. Well, she was having none of that. Doris Reeves was hers, she and her unborn baby; they walked in her dreams, and asked for justice. '*The dead have no rights*.' Maybe not, but Sarah had a right to know the truth, having gone so far in search of it. Truth was not reserved for the police, who would follow it so far and then lose interest if the language of priorities took them off in another direction. Sarah had no such priorities. She would follow truth to the end, or at least as far as she could.

Nevertheless, the Inspector was probably right to this extent, that it would be unwise for her to go about her task so openly. The parish register was available to more people than the police. Now Sarah thought of it, she didn't need the parish register: there was a wooden tablet on the wall of the church, giving the names of all the parish priests since 1823. After that, to someone familiar with the publications of the Crime Club, the next step was obvious. *Crockford's Clerical Directory* would be on the telephone.

Already her decision to find out what had happened to the vicar's wife had ceased to be a mere matter of interest. Sarah Arnott, née Bridges, her head wreathed with serpents, had joined the company of the Eumenides.

It was easy. There were minor hitches, but it was easy.

The wooden tablet in the church told her that James Elroy Partridge had been parish priest from 1940 to 1953. Nowadays, Sarah knew, the vicar had to shuttle between four parishes, serving Holy Communion at one, then driving six miles to conduct a brisk Matins at another: there was a chart in the porch to let the congregation know where he could be found on any Sunday. But back in the 1940s, James Elroy Partridge had ministered to this one village only. Why would he suddenly have acquired a second car? If the Partridges had not been a two-car family before, why would they become one in the summer of 1948?

The vicar's wife had bought the car from Doris Reeves. What was the connection between them? Miss Hedges had said that Dorrie lodged at the vicarage. Having decided to sell the car, she would have offered it first to her landlady, who wanted one, or – more probably – she had mentioned her intention to sell it and the vicar's wife had jumped in first with an offer she couldn't refuse. Why? Miss Hedges had said quite clearly that she thought the purchase odd; in pointing so deliberately to the oddity she was pointing, as far as she was prepared to do so, in the direction of the murderer. And it *was* odd. Natural to buy a cheap car from one's lodger, who had no further use for it, but odd that the vendor, heavy with child and burdened by at least two suitcases, had preferred to make a journey by country bus, train and then bus again to her home in Nottingham instead of putting herself and her luggage into the Morris Eight, driving it back home and selling it there. Where would the vicar's wife have found the money? Miss Hedges had said that Dorrie had bought the car for twopence (probably twenty pounds or so at that time), but even so, back in 1948, if a second car was required the husband bought it because the wife had no money of her own, and even a twopenny car would cost a bit to run.

It occurred to Sarah that her own car had been bought with Simon's money, or at least from the joint account, which came to the same thing since she herself was not earning these days.

If Sarah had been Dorrie Reeves, and determined for some reason not yet discovered to sell her car before leaving the village, she would at least have insisted that the vicar's wife drove her to the station – in which case the vicar's wife would know that Dorrie had left, so that the skeleton by Garbett's Barn could not be hers. But it was hers. Sarah knew it was hers, and so did the Inspector, who would have to go through the process of checking the dental records, but must know as well as she that two young women, both eight months pregnant, both disappearing from the same village at the same time, was too much of a coincidence. The next step must be to find the vicar's wife and grill her. How old would she be by now?

Would she be dead? It would be horribly anti-climactic if she were. She must not be dead.

Crockford's. She tried Directory Enquiries, but *Crockford's Clerical Directory* was not listed in London. She drove with Jonathan to Leamington Spa, parked the car in the multi-storey car park, and took Jonathan in the sling to the Reference Library. This was the new sling, which was worn like a rucksack on the back; he had grown too heavy for the old sling. She was not too happy about using the new sling amongst crowds, because, being no longer in her sight, he might be plucked out of the rucksack by some baby-snatcher – they worked in teams, these people, one of them in front distracting her attention while the other whipped Jonathan away into a waiting pram and off down the street at the speed of light. But there was a flight of stone stairs to the Reference Library, and Sarah was not sure she would be able to get his pushchair up it: the Detective Inspector and his investigating team, she supposed, would never be required to make this kind of decision.

Crockford's Directory was found for her by a helpful librarian, who also made a space where Jonathan might safely sit. It appeared that Crockford was not the publisher, but just a name to put on the book, like Old Moore on the Almanac; maybe it was all a piece of clerical mystification, and there never had been a Crockford. The *Directory* was part of the publishing empire of the Church Commissioners in Great Smith Street. Sarah picked Jonathan up again, and drove home by way of the superstore, where she bought, among other nourishing comestibles, Purée of Creamed Celery with Gravy, to which he had lately shown himself partial.

She phoned the Church Commissioners in the afternoon. A wary young man on the exchange put her through to General Enquiries, whence she was passed through four different offices, ending with a male voice which was three parts curiosity to one part unction. He took down the few details she was able, and chose, to give – Sarah was convinced that she could hear a quill pen scratching as he wrote – and promised to phone her back, which he did within the hour.

'I'm afraid Mr Partridge has passed away.'

'How old was he?'

'I'm sorry?'

If the vicar was dead, it was probable that his wife would be dead also. There had been nothing on the wooden tablet by which one could guess whether James Elroy Partridge had been at the beginning or near the close of his ministry. Sarah said, 'Did he pass away at an advanced age? In the fullness of years?'

'If your interest is in finding him, I don't see that the age at which he died is of any great relevance.' To the one part helpfulness was added an equal part of being put upon. 'I suppose I may be able to find out.'

'It's really his wife I'm trying to find. I suppose I should have mentioned that.'

'Yes, I suppose you should.'

'She was an old schoolfriend of my mother's. Now my mother's dying – in a hospice, you know – and keeps asking for her.' Could anyone believe this rubbish? And if one's wicked lies came true – as had been said to Sarah when she was a child – was Sarah's mother now in danger of contracting a mortal illness?

The voice became warmer, curiosity being replaced by concern. Sarah felt a pang of guilt. 'I'll see what we can manage. I don't have the date of birth, I'm afraid, so . . . Ah! Yes. . . . He died in harness, that is to say before retirement, while still ministering. Nineteen eighty-two. He must have been under sixty-five then, so there is a chance – a good chance, I should say – that his wife may still be alive.'

'Where?'

'Where would she be living now? I'm afraid I have no idea. Obviously no longer in the parsonage. I can transfer you to another department which deals with relicts – widows or young children, you know, requiring support – charitable cases – and she'd have a pension, a widow's pension, bound to: there'd be a record in that department, though the Commissioners are never very keen to give out any information to do with money.'

'Where's the parish where he died? She'd have had friends there. She may have found somewhere local to live.'

'Yes, she may. How very sharp of you! I agree: it's certainly worth a try. Melthwaite. It's a little village in Cumbria. You could try writing to the present incumbent. He's bound to know: she'd be one of his parishioners.'

She decided not to talk to Simon about it. He had been insensitive recently to her concern with the dead girl and her baby, even impatient. To do him justice, this was not like Simon. Usually he would put on a show of interest: she would watch him putting it on like an overtired junior doctor putting on his white coat for yet another avoidable emergency. Once upon a time, she supposed, the interest would have been genuine, back in the early days when Sarah had not yet assumed the role of wife and mother, and Simon, being at a more junior level, had not taken his job so seriously. Since then Promotions had taken hold of him like some cancer, eating up discrimination, objectivity, moderation and most of all his sense of humour about a line of work which was so essentially trivial – except, Simon would now say, that it was not trivial to them, since it paid the bills.

He couldn't see it these days, couldn't see what was important and what was not. 'Why do you have to go to Dresden to decide which plastic animal to give away in a pack?' Sarah would ask, and Simon would launch patiently into a reply which always began with the words, 'It's not a question of'. So now Sarah had ceased to ask such questions. She and Simon rarely talked about his job any more; it was too complicated. Even now, when there was a crisis in Promotions, they did not discuss its nature. It seemed to Sarah that they rarely talked about anything at all any more.

She had seen it coming, but in London she had been able

to keep it at bay, since Simon had not then had to leave home so early and get back so late. They had visited friends and done things together, gone to movies and the theatre, eaten out, taken evening classes in Italian in preparation for a Tuscan holiday, driven into the country together looking for a weekend cottage, and found Garbett's Barn. She had seen it coming, and then Jonathan had come, not accidentally (except inasmuch as it had taken longer for Sarah to become pregnant than they had thought), but a planned baby, to be cherished and perhaps followed by another when they could afford it. And at first her pregnancy and its progress, and then the birth, had been absorbing for Simon as well as for Sarah – well, not *as* absorbing, since it was not his body which was changing and anyway he still had to go out to work, but absorbing during their own time together, and totally absorbing as a topic of conversation and concern.

Then they had moved out of London altogether, or at least Sarah and Jonathan had, and Sarah could not regret that: she wanted to live in the country, and would have hated to return to London. But Simon's concern for Jonathan had diminished sharply, since he now saw so little of him, getting his own breakfast before leaving the house at seven while Sarah was occupied with Jonathan's first change and bottle, and often returning (what with the crisis in Promotions) after Jonathan had been put to bed. At weekends he would put the concern back on again, but it seemed to Sarah to be like the houseman's white coat. He did not play with Jonathan as she played, not wholeheartedly for the pleasure of it, but as a duty.

Memory plays tricks. She began to question whether she and Simon had really been so easy with each other during the early days. She asked him, 'When we were first married, when we were living together, what did we talk about?'

He couldn't remember. 'Something, I suppose. We

weren't Trappist monks: we used to chat away. What does anybody talk about? Politics? The weather? Cost of living? Probably your mother.'

'We never talk nowadays.'

'What else are we doing at this moment?'

If you loved someone, you didn't keep making debating points. No, she wouldn't tell him about the vicar's wife; she didn't want to, didn't feel like it. That meant that she would have to go north to the village in Cumbria over a couple of days when Simon was away at one of his conferences, or stopping overnight at the flat. What with the crisis in Promotions, that should be soon enough. How long would it take to drive to Cumbria – four hours? By herself she might drive up and back in a day and still have time to talk to Mrs Partridge, but Jonathan could not be left, and taking him with her would slow her down. She would have to find a hotel for the night; that shouldn't be difficult. If Simon phoned during this period, he would get no answer and that might worry him, but it would do him good to worry about his own family for a change.

Simon said, 'What would you like to talk about? Your investigation? How's it going?'

Sarah said, 'I've been taken off the case.'

That night she dreamed two dreams, one following the other, which had no sense in them. Strictly speaking they were not dreams at all, but pictures, flashes from dreams of which the remainder had been lost.

There was a young woman, kneeling on the pavement of a city street. Her knitted hat was pulled down low over her forehead; she wore metal spectacles and an overcoat made out of a grey blanket. She was weeping, holding both hands in woollen mittens up to her face to hide it. Blood and tears ran down from her eyes. And the second picture was at the periphery of the dreamer's vision – of Sarah's vision – where, on a scrubbed pine table, a child's fluffy toy, a leopard, twitched like a dog in death agony.

What did they mean? They didn't mean anything. The young woman was not Doris Reeves, nothing like her; she was of the 1990s, probably a protester at some demo. '*We dream about ourselves, Sarah Arnott.*' So who was Sarah supposed to be – the leopard? They did not buy such toys for Jonathan, who was not old enough for them and would not be for at least a year.

Obviously she must not give the vicar's wife any warning: there must be no time to cobble together an explanation. Therefore the Crockford man's suggestion of writing to the present vicar to ask whether his predecessor's widow still lived in the village would not do, because if she did, he would mention the letter to Mrs Partridge and the name of the village from which that letter came might sound alarm bells. Equally obviously it would be foolish to make the journey without being sure that its object would actually be there at the end. Answer: British Telecom's Directory Enquiries. The woman would have to be on the telephone. Vicars' wives spend half their lives on the telephone, and old habits die hard. If there were a subscriber named Partridge living at or somewhere not far from Melthwaite, it would be worth the journey. If not, Sarah would think again.

There was a Partridge. She would take her chance, and go. The occasion came soon. A six o'clock, open-ended meeting about Marketing Strategy, at which Simon was required to make a presentation from the promotional angle, would keep him in London over a Wednesday night. The words, 'I thought I might drive north, and take Jonathan with me,' attempted to form themselves into a pattern which would not lead to an argument and Sarah's being made to feel foolish, but failed, and so remained unuttered; she would explain, if explanation were required, after their return.

On the Tuesday morning, she consulted maps and a tourist guide. Penrith seemed to be the nearest town of any consequence. She phoned a hotel of middling size, and was refused.

'But you're a reputable hotel; you've got stars in the Guide. You must have facilities for babies.'

'For children, madam, of course. This is an area of natural beauty. We have families come touring; we have an excellent reputation for family holidays. We do children's portions in the restaurant, and put up two cots in any double room without charge. We're well accustomed to children, and well-provided with facilities for same. But people with very young babies don't usually travel.'

He meant 'respectable people'; he must think her a gypsy. Sarah said, 'Look, I'm quite respectable – married and all that.' She wondered whether having a mother in the BBC would make a difference. 'I can provide references.'

'It's not a question of respectability, I do assure you. But most of our holidaymakers go in for all-weather outdoor pursuits. Fell-walking and such. Fishing. A small baby would be out of place. And, as I say, we really haven't the facilities.'

'He doesn't need facilities; I bring them with me. He sleeps in his carrycot, and I feed him myself.' She could hear the intake of breath at the other end of the phone. The man imagined that she would breastfeed in the breakfast room. 'I'd make up his bottle in the bedroom. All I need is an electric kettle.'

But it did no good. She was refused by three hotels. The subtext, she decided, was a fear that Jonathan would cry all night and disturb the other guests. Finally she found a place where the manager, summoned to the phone by a desk clerk whom she had managed to rattle by threatening to complain to the Tourist Board, agreed to accommodate them both in the annexe. It was not a good start.

On the Wednesday morning she did not allow Jonathan to sleep after his seven o'clock bottle, but kept him awake until it was time to feed and change him again just before starting out. She packed a suitcase, found a green plastic carrier bag with a Harrods' label as a guarantee of affluence, if not of respectability, and filled it with the baby gear, loaded these with the travel cot and pushchair into her car, and strapped Jonathan into his baby seat. Then she locked the house, leaving a note for Elsie (who had her own key) on the kitchen table, and drove north.

She had it all planned, and generally speaking the plan worked. Four hours for the journey. Jonathan would sleep for the first two, and did. By the time he woke, they would be on the motorway, and Sarah should have fifteen minutes to find a service station before he began grizzling. So it was. Service stations, unlike hotels in areas of natural beauty, have facilities for babies. In their ladies' toilets, there are changing rooms in which babies may be changed and fed. Sarah changed Jonathan and fed him, decided not to push her luck by feeding herself in the Granary self-service, and bought a couple of chocolate bars in the shop instead to eat in the car; they were comfort food, she knew, and her behaviour grossly self-indulgent, and she did try never to eat sweets in front of Jonathan in case he were to copy her in later life, but there was, as the Inspector would have said, a language of priorities in this case. She was back on the motorway within half an hour, while Jonathan slept again. By two o'clock they had reached the hotel, which was some way outside Penrith, on the wrong side for Melthwaite but not far enough to matter.

It seemed to have been converted from a farmhouse. The annexe, she guessed, had been a byre, but was now divided into two rooms, each with its own front door, like two little semi-detached houses. Her room had high stone walls, plastered and painted white on the inside, wooden beams and a false ceiling to block off where the hayloft would have been. Even if Jonathan were to cry in the night (and he never did), the occupants of the room next door would not be troubled, the stone wall between was so thick.

The room was large, with a sofa, desk and armchairs as well as a bed, and with a bathroom en-suite. There were flowers on the mantel above the Magicoal electric fire, and a dish of fruit on the coffee table with a glass of sweet sherry and two almond biscuits in a saucer. Sarah warmed to it. It was remarkably pleasant, if one forgot the sweet sherry, and cheap at the price.

The manager himself had conducted her to the room, making it clear that he was personally responsible for the flowers, the glass of sherry and the fruit. He considered her an honoured guest, he said; he had the highest regard for motherhood, and often asked himself where we would all be without mothers. He had obviously been affected by her threat to complain to the Tourist Board, and was particularly anxious to give satisfaction; consequently Sarah put herself out, in so far as time allowed, to be cordial. She wondered if he owned the hotel as well as managing it, and had carried out the conversion himself when he discovered that farming had ceased to pay, but he did not look like someone who had once been a farmer. No, this was a man who, unsure of his metier, had been guided by a school Careers Officer into the catering trade, who had picked his way through two years at a polytechnic and three jobs, each a step upwards on the careers ladder, always so determined to please that he had no idea whether he himself was pleased by what he was doing, and had ended up in his thirties still just as unsure, but with the realisation that it was now too late to change. He had a long freckled face, with thinning red hair combed straight back to reveal a bumpy forehead. His arms were long also, long and thin, too long for his body, and his hands too large for his arms. His elbows were so sharp that Sarah wondered whether they came to a point. He would be a dangerous partner in bed. If he slept about promiscuously, there must be women all over Penrith with deep wounds where the manager had injudiciously placed an elbow at some moment of sexual frenzy. But he did not look like someone who slept about; he had a married look. She supposed that he might have to have his jackets specially made for him, except that clearly they were not bespoke. In fact, if one looked closely, one could see where his wife had extended the sleeves.

'We've a little lad of our own,' he said, baring his teeth at Jonathan. 'Older than yours; he's three. I'm told I've quite an affinity with children. You have to be young at heart as you go through life, don't you?'

This was all very welcoming, but could not be allowed to go on. The time was already two-thirty by the electric clock set into one wall, and Melthwaite twelve miles on the other side of town by country roads. Sarah said, 'You're very kind, but I'm afraid I'll have to ask you to excuse me. It's been a long journey, and I still have to feed and change the baby. He gets very tiresome if he's kept waiting. You know how they are at this age.'

The manager did know how they were, only too well did he know, Mrs Arnott (he had been taught always to remember the names of guests; it makes such a difference), and he took his leave instanter. If there was anything she required, she had only to ask. Dinner was a moveable feast between seven p.m. and nine, and in case of emergency, she could always ask for a toasted sandwich in the room.

The door closed behind him. Sarah looked at her watch. Two thirty-five. Jonathan's bedtime was eight. It would take her at least an hour to unpack, boil a kettle for the bottle, get him fed, and settle him for the next part of the journey. They would arrive at Melthwaite after four, and must then find the house, and be away again by six. It didn't seem long for the process of grilling the vicar's wife.

Would it be better to wait, and go next morning? No; there would still be problems of time, when one considered the length of the journey home. Anyway, she was in the mood; she was raring to go. She went into the en-suite bathroom to fill the kettle, and looked at herself in the mirror over the washbasin. 'God, Sarah Arnott!' she said, 'You're irresistible when you're like this.'

Country roads in Warwickshire are hazardous because the young farmers drive round blind corners at sixty miles an hour. In Cumbria the hazards seemed to be more orographical. She turned off the B5305 and found herself driving on what should have been single-track roads (except that vans, lorries, even a school bus, came the other way), winding between steep banks at impossible angles up hills and down into valleys where the rivers were crossed by narrow hump-backed bridges. She arrived in Melthwaite later than she had hoped, tired and cross, with Jonathan grizzling in the back.

The village was roughly a third of the way up one of the steeper hills. Stone houses and a church, a shop and the Village Hall were set about a crossroads, in the middle of which was a drinking fountain with a metal cup on a chain and a tablet commemorating the dead of two wars; it was clearly a hazard to traffic, and bore its scars proudly. The address given for 'Partridge L' in the telephone directory was 'Troutbeck View' with no street name, but it should be easy to find, and was: a wooden sign on the wall of the shop-cum-Post-Office read 'Troutbeck View Holiday Apartments', and pointed downhill to the river.

It was a square solidly built house of three storeys, the doors and window-frames much in need of paint, with a neglected front garden and a large board on which the words 'HOLIDAY APARTMENTS' had been painted, bright red on light blue, some time ago. Sarah parked the car outside, transferred Jonathan from baby seat to carrycot, and went to knock on the front door, which was answered by a middle-aged Welsh woman in a state of disarray.

'A room, is it? We don't do B-and-B as a rule, but as it happens, we have a vacancy.'

'Does Mrs Partridge live here?'

The woman looked from Sarah to Jonathan and back again, trying to assess the situation. If Sarah were a relation, she would know well enough that Mrs Partridge lived there, and would not need to ask. If she were a social worker, bailiff or something legal, she would not bring a baby with her, and anyway her accent was not local. A strange young woman with a baby might be thought to be a paternity matter, but Mrs Partridge was female and a senior citizen. (Did she have a son, Sarah wondered. Grandchildren? Was there a covey of tiny Partridges?) The silence grew between them. The woman would give nothing away.

Sarah said, 'I'm Mrs Arnott. She doesn't know me.'

'Ah!' An upper lip chewed thoughtfully. Not a paternity matter, then, but most options were still open. 'I'm at sixes and sevens at the moment, to tell you the truth,' the woman said. 'In the summer, things get on top of you.'

This could take for ever, and there was so little time. Sarah said, 'I'm not a debt-collector or anything. I'm from a village where her husband used to be the vicar. I've come a long way to ask her some questions about . . . about church affairs. I had to bring my baby with me, because . . . .' It was a moment for inspiration if she was to get past Cerberus. '. . . because my husband's away at the moment at a conference in Dunedin, and my mother's doing a Christmas Spectular for the BBC.'

The woman's mistrust melted like a choc-ice on a sunny Bank Holiday. 'Oh, BBC, is it? Top floor. I can't ask you to go straight up, because it's Christian Fellowship on a

Wednesday, but it won't take long; there's so few of them these days.'

'But her husband's dead, I thought.'

'That's right. Angina – very tragic. He fell down the steps of the pulpit after the benediction, and died in the vestry. But she always used to take the Fellowship; that wasn't his area of interest, you see. And they're used to going to her, so she carries on. Gives her something to do. I'll make a cup of tea, and they'll be down directly. I'm Chapel myself, always have been, but I don't go these days because it's too far.'

They were not down directly. Sarah fielded the woman's interested questions for twenty minutes while Jonathan grizzled, and nothing could be done about that because she had not brought a bottle or any of his formula. One of the Crime Club detectives would have used the time to gain information about Mrs Partridge from the Welsh woman, but there seemed to be little to gain. She had moved out of the vicarage when her husband died, and, having no capital but only a small pension and no children or other close relatives who might have taken her in, had moved into one of the holiday apartments as a permanent resident on a special rate, with the understanding that, if they were fully booked in August, she would find somewhere else for that month. This August, as it happened, because of the recession they were not fully booked; Sarah was lucky to find her.

At last the Christian Fellowship was over, and 'they' came down, five old women and two old men, moving slowly and watching their feet on the stairs. The Welsh woman offered to look after Jonathan, but admitted that she was unused to babies, having had none of her own, and he let out a howl when she picked him up, so Sarah had to take him upstairs with her, still howling. Mrs Partridge was at her open door, wondering about the noise, as they approached. She said, 'Let me take him.'

Mysteriously, in spite of never having been exposed to

anyone of great-grandmotherly age, Jonathan stopped crying while held by Mrs Partridge. Sarah said, 'Thank you,' to the Welsh woman, who went reluctantly downstairs again to her state of disarray. Mrs Partridge said, 'Should I know you, my dear? Have you come for Fellowship?.

'I've come from Radcote.'

Silence. *'That's what I used to tell the children. Always count to five before answering.'* Then, 'I remember Radcote.'

'We live on the hill above the village. Garbett's Barn – it wasn't a house in your day.' Remember the Inspector. Pause. Watch for a reaction. But Mrs Partridge was looking down at the baby in her arms and crooning at him, and whatever she may have remembered about Garbett's Barn, she gave nothing away.

Hit her with it. 'Doris Reeves' skeleton was discovered buried on our land six weeks ago.'

Silence again. Sarah found herself counting inside her head . . . ten . . . fifteen . . . twenty.

'Doris Reeves went back to her mother in Nottingham.'

'No.'

'That's what she said.'

'She never went. Somebody murdered her.'

'Are you from the police?' She looked up, her expression mild, still redolent of Christian Fellowship. 'You'd better take your baby back.'

Sarah took Jonathan, who at once became fretful again, but she held him firmly. 'I'm not from the police. I'm an interested party; that's all. Miss Hedges told me you bought her car. Why?'

'Miss Hedges? How is she now?'

'She's in an old folks' Home at Glazeby. Why did you buy Doris Reeves's car?'

'She needed the money.'

'Sorry?'

'There was a baby coming? Did you know that?' Sarah nodded. The time to hit Mrs Partridge with the baby's skeleton, curled up within its mother's pelvis, was not yet. She would do that, when she needed to provoke another reaction, not that hitting Mrs Partridge with unwelcome information had done much good so far. 'Dorrie had no money, and her mother was unlikely to give her any. They didn't get on. She needed money for the baby, and had nothing to sell but her car.'

'She could have used it to get her back to Nottingham, and sold it there.'

A wan smile. The woman was insufferably gentle. 'Oh, I don't think so. Who would have bought it? It was in a very poor state, you know. Steve Dast at the garage used to coax it to go, but never for long or for far. It might be worth something now, of course – they have these Rallies, don't they? But not then.'

'So why did you buy it?'

'I told you; she needed the money. Dorrie was a proud girl. She wouldn't have taken money from me; she knew I had none. But I persuaded James – my husband – to buy the car. Some of the money was our own, but some came from church expenses and some from the poor box. Thirty-six pounds. I don't think she'd paid as much as that for it herself, and she'd had it two years. It was really undriveable, Dorrie's car, no use to anyone, but it would have been unkind to remind her of that.'

'If the car was undriveable, what did you do with it?'

'Drained out the petrol and left it at the bottom of the garden; it may still be there. The schoolchildren used to play in it, and I think it may have been used for lessons – projects and that sort of thing. Stevie Dast cannibalised bits of the engine and paid for them by doing bits of maintenance on our own car. So many aspects of clergy life in those days – in the villages at least – were a matter of barter. I expect they still are.'

'The baby's skeleton was found inside her own, curled up. She was eight months pregnant.'

Silence. To be expected. Fifteen . . . twenty . . . twenty-five.

'We all knew she was pregnant. She went back to Nottingham to have the baby.'

'Did you see her go? Did you drive her to the station at Leamington? She lodged at your house. Who saw her leave the village, and how did she go?'

Twenty . . . twenty-five . . . thirty. Mrs Partridge's hands were moving, the fingers rubbing each other as if for warmth on this August day. 'The children at the school gave her a card they'd made themselves, bluebirds and flowers, all carefully drawn and coloured with crayons. I'm afraid I'm a little tired now. The Fellowship takes it out of one, though it's a great comfort too, of course. I think perhaps you should leave. Your baby's overtired.'

Sarah looked at her watch. It was true that she should be going, true that Jonathan was overtired. 'I'll come back tomorrow morning.'

'I'd rather you didn't.'

Was this it? A brush-off? The CID would never have accepted it; they would have pulled Mrs Partridge in to assist them with their enquiries. But Sarah was only an interested party; she had no official standing in this affair and would have to leave when she was told. Was there any one thing she ought to try to find out before she went? Of course! 'Do you know who the father was?' she said.

'It was none of my business. Doris never told me, and I certainly never asked.'

'But did you know?' A quick shake of the head, which might have meant anything from 'Don't push me!' to a nervous tic.

'Did she come back to the vicarage that night before she left? Did she sleep in her room? What happened to her luggage? Tell me, please, did you actually see her leave?'

'Please go.'

The Welsh woman was at the foot of the stairs, looking up. Mrs Partridge stood at her open door, and said, 'I have an excellent memory, though the names of flowers do evade me, and sometimes of people. Sometimes I mislay my shopping-list; that's of no consequence, since I have very little shopping to do, and it's not far to go. Mrs Bowen-Davis is very kind; she helps to keep me up to the mark. I manage remarkably well, all things considered. What I dread is senility; I have seen so much of it in my parish work. I should like you to remember that. The old do not fear death. They may welcome it, particularly those of us who are assured, by our Saviour's grace, of life everlasting. Goodbye. I'm sorry I shall not be in if you call again.'

Six o'clock. Jonathan must be fed, he must be changed, and twelve miles on these roads took longer than she had planned. Later, in reflection and in calm, she must try to evaluate what she had found out, but she already knew that it was very little, by no means enough. She had made a right cock-up of it, if the truth were told.

At four-thirty next morning, shortly after dawn, the hotel manager came to her room. He was wearing a tracksuit and trainers, and he was sweating. He said, 'I just popped in to make sure the little fellow was okay.'

Sarah said, 'Go away!' and the manager came closer and stood beside the bed. It was strange to see him. Sweat gathered in beads on his forehead, overflowed from some reservoir behind his ears, ran down the side of his face and splashed off his chin, yet he was shivering violently. He said, 'I've got nothing on under this tracksuit, you know.'

'Go back to bed. Your wife will miss you.'

'She thinks I'm out running. It's the only time I can get away, in the early morning. I like to keep fit.'

Luckily so far there had not been a peep out of Jonathan. She knew that she should be afraid, and at some level she was, but at least on the surface there was too much anger to leave room for fear. She said, 'Go away! I'm not interested.'

'I'm stronger than you are. I could force you, not that I ever would.'

'You think I won't complain?'

'Who'd believe you? It's only your word against mine?' His enormous hands hung twitching at the ends of wrists which the arms of his tracksuit were not long enough to cover. He looked like something out of *Alice In Wonderland* or science fiction, half man, half stick-insect. 'I'm still young,' he said. 'I've got my youth. You want me, don't you? You're a defenceless woman. I represent strength to you.' It must be true that he had nothing on under the tracksuit, since an enormous erection, unconfined by Y-fronts, was manifest and far too close.

The hotel manager noticed the direction of her gaze, and it seemed to give him courage, though he continued to shiver. 'You can take it any way you like,' he said. 'I'm not fussy.'

The fear beneath the anger began to rise towards the surface. For her own sake, for Jonathan's sake, she must not show it, must not lose the initiative, must not allow him to move in on her. She concentrated on keeping her voice steady. Cool, Sarah: dead cool, girl! Don't move until you must, and then move quickly. She said, 'Do you do this sort of thing often?'

'Never. Never before. It was you being on your own with the baby turned me on.'

'I'm afraid I don't believe you.' It was time for the quick move. He was standing next to the bedside table on which there was a telephone. 'Let's ask the night porter, shall we?' She reached quickly, easily, across him, and picked up the telephone. As she did so, he moved towards her so that her arm brushed the front of his erection, and he cried out as if in pain.

Was it pain or was it ecstasy? Did he believe that she had touched him deliberately? Get on with it, Sarah. Don't pause to find out. But she was her mother's daughter. 'What's the matter?'

'I've come. Oh Christ, I've come!'

She replaced the receiver. 'Well, now you've come, you'd better go.'

He stood there, holding the front of his track-suit trousers with both hands, his eyes closed. 'Aaah!' he said, 'Aaaaah!' She waited. 'You won't tell anyone?'

'I won't tell anyone.'

'You're a good sort, I'll say that. For a woman.' He was on his way to the door.

'I don't want to see you again before I leave.'

'You won't. I'll be doing the rounds. There's trouble in the kitchen. We're understaffed. It never stops.'

As the door closed behind the hotel manager, Jonathan woke, demanding immediate attention. Sarah picked him up. 'If it's not one thing, it's another,' Sarah said to her son. Then she held him closely to her, and first began to tremble as violently as the hotel manager had done, and then to weep, but of course that did no good; it only set Jonathan off, and she had to stop in order to console him.

The journey home was not as easy as the journey out had been, because Jonathan had decided that he disliked travelling, and comfort stops had to be made at several service stations. Nevertheless, by the time Simon showed up that evening, all was much as usual at Garbett's Barn.

Simon did not mention that he had phoned the night before and found nobody at home, so Sarah did not have to explain her absence since no explanation was being demanded. She would not have lied to her husband; she would have told the truth about her visit to Mrs Partridge and endured his ridicule, even his impatience with her. A part of her had hoped that she and Simon might have talked over the experience together, that he would have helped her to consider critically what had been said and what had not been said. They would have done so once. Simon had a good analytical mind and might have enjoyed exercising it on a problem which had nothing to do with bloody Promotions. Still, if he hadn't even bothered to phone . . .

Except that he must have phoned; of course he had phoned, he always phoned, so why didn't he say so? Since she never went out, and he knew it, why didn't he ask her where she had been? Could he be nursing jealous suspicions like Othello? Paranoid jealousy had figured often in the Crime Club stories as a motive for murder, and usually of wives. She had better speak and put a stop to it before it bloomed.

'You didn't phone last night.'

'No, the meeting went on a bit and I stopped off to get something to eat and got back rather late. I thought you'd probably be in bed.'

'I might have worried about you.'

'You knew where I was.'

After that it was impossible to tell him. In this matter of Doris Reeves and the vicar's wife, she was on her own. The woman had never said that she saw Dorrie leave, or that anyone had done so. She had dodged the question. Was that because, as a committed Christian, she was trying not to lie? If so, she would have told the truth whenever she could; most of what she had been willing to say would have been true. Was what she had said about the car the truth? – it was certainly circumstantial. Would Dorrie's car, perhaps, still be at the bottom of the vicarage garden, overgrown by nettles and convolvulus? Who lived at the vicarage now? – media people, she'd heard, something to do with local interest programmes in the Central region: she supposed that they must be feeling the breeze, now

LATIN

She sent a message to Miss Hedges at Temple Glazeby that she would come on Wednesday, Elsie's day: she still did not fancy taking Jonathan with her to the Home. She did not know what to make of the message. 'Made away with herself': that had to mean suicide, but why? No accusation had been made, no pressure brought upon Mrs Partridge, who, if one were keeping score, had come much the better out of the exchange.

This suicide was in the wrong place; it should come at the end as part of the denouement. *'The game's up, Carruthers. You'll find a revolver and a bottle of whisky in the library.'* It was so unfair; it was like a criticism. Sarah had never suggested that the vicar's wife herself had killed her lodger; that wasn't in the least likely. All she had said – she could remember clearly – was, 'Did you see her leave? Did anyone see her leave?' It must be something to do with that bloody Morris Eight. Had there been no other way for the Partridges to provide Doris with money except by buying a car for which they had no use? Was it still there, rusting at the bottom of their garden?

'What do you feel about war crimes?' She did not wish to think that her visit to the vicar's wife, undertaken in no more than the spirit of detached enquiry, might for some unknown reason have caused the woman to kill herself.

Therefore she would not think of it. It was nothing to do with her, not her responsibility. She discovered – as she was bound to discover – that she could not help thinking about it. Doris Reeves, babyless, bounded down the road from London to Brighton, driving a vintage car. She wore leathers, tweeds and a headscarf, and bared her teeth in triumph at the spectators watching in the rain. The hotel manager sat by her side, depressed. Sarah awoke, tense, her fingers clenched, and pushed at Simon. 'Turn over on your side. You're keeping me awake.' He was not snoring, but one had to do something.

She wondered whether she ought to tell the Inspector about Miss Hedges's message, but not for long. If Mrs Partridge really had committed suicide as a result of Sarah's visit, then Sarah might be held responsible, particularly since she had been told to say and do nothing more in this affair. Better to keep quiet, at least until she had been to see Miss Hedges. The police were great ones for apportioning blame; she preferred not to give the Inspector the satisfaction of blaming her until she was sure she deserved it.

Seven elderly persons, five women and two men, moving slowly and watching their feet on the stairs. They would be without Fellowship now. Sarah's fault. Responsibility stretched further than one could ever see.

The vicar's wife had reached out for Jonathan and he had become quiet at once, allowing her to hold him. Could that gentle old woman really have killed herself? How? And how did Miss Hedges come to know of it?

Tuesday was garden maintenance day. Jeremy came up himself instead of Clyde to monitor progress. He would be bound to know about the vicarage garden. Jeremy knew about all the village gardens. It was habitual with him to cast a professional eye over them as he went about, disapproving of what had been done or – worse – neglected.

Sarah found him misting tomatoes in the conservatory. The tomatoes had been cropping abundantly, but many of them split, and a mould grew in the cracks unless they were quickly picked and eaten. Sarah had grown tired of split tomatoes, and longed for a whole one. 'You've been over-watering, haven't you?' Jeremy said.

'Probably.'

'Over-watering and over-feeding, I'd say, and both irregular; they're bound to split. Little and often; that's the way with tomatoes.'

She had been warned not to ask questions in the village, but Jeremy was different; he had achieved socially upward mobility and become almost a Yuppie. Also he enjoyed imparting information. Sarah said, 'Do you know anything about an old Morris Eight in the vicarage garden?'

'What, that old thing?' She waited for him to add, 'Civil War Rubbish!' but of course he didn't. Instead he asked, 'How do you know about that?'

Once again she had been pushed onto the defensive. The detectives of the Crime Club series never had this problem. Investigators were keen and thrusting, suspects were defensive; that was the way of it in fiction, but not, it seemed, in the agricultural Midlands.

Sarah was discovering also that one of the major problems in detection was remembering what people were supposed to know. The skeleton had not yet been officially identified, but if the police had been asking questions about Doris Reeves in the village most of the older villagers would have tumbled to it. In particular, the person or persons who had killed and/or buried her would know that a provisional identification had been made, and would have become alarmed. What was known to the older would soon spread to the younger villagers, but this knowledge would mean little to those who were younger than forty, or had arrived during the last forty years and had never met Doris Reeves. The older villagers would know that the

Morris Eight had once belonged to Dorrie, and might be suspicious of questions about it, but Jeremy, still in his early twenties and by no stretch of the deductive imagination a suspect, would not know who had once owned the car or who Dorrie herself had been, so he might be safely questioned if she could think of a credible excuse for questioning him. 'Simon mentioned it,' she said. 'There's a friend of his in the office goes in for vintage cars. He wondered if it could be restored.'

'Belongs on a tip.' It was clear that the presence of a rusty car in a garden rankled with someone who had studied the designs of Gertrude Jekyll. 'They call it a feature. Clematis montana grown all over it. Consequently you can't see it. Best thing, if you ask me, but what's the point of a feature you can't see?'

'How long has it been there?'

'God knows. Kids from the school used to play in it until one of them cut his leg.'

'Did you ever play in it?'

He shook his head. 'Better things to do.' Jeremy would always have better things to do; he seemed to be without vices. Sarah had a brief urge to reach out and touch the golden fuzz on his chest where the checked shirt was unbuttoned, to wind the hair round her fingers, and so draw him slowly towards her. The urged passed. Jeremy said, 'Water from the bottom, earlier the better, about halfway up the saucer, no more. Leave them alone in the evening, unless it's been very hot, and they're dry; they don't like wet feet overnight. Feed every other day. And don't let the temperature in here go above the mid-eighties or you'll get greenback.'

She could not say she was sexually unsatisfied, no question of that. Simon was extremely conscientious about his marital duties. He said that, once marriage had settled down into a routine, one had better make sure that sex was part of that routine, otherwise it tended to get neglected.

Never rely, said Simon, on the sudden moment of desire, but set a regular day and time. In their case, Mondays to Fridays were impossible, because he was always tired from work and travel, so it had to be weekends, and afternoons were better then evenings. Sunday afternoons had too many vulgar associations, so it had to be Saturdays; when Jonathan was older and capable of wandering into bedrooms unannounced, they would have to think again. Meanwhile Saturday afternoons it was – regularly – unless Simon were summoned overseas or to a weekend conference at the company training centre in Huntingdon, in which case he would leave work early during the week and make it up to her.

Sarah supposed that Simon must be right, and that marriages did settle into a routine; they were bound to do so. She didn't see many other married couples these days, and her parents' marriage had ended when she was five and her father went off to live with Gladys, whom Sarah had never been able to bring herself to like. She and Simon had begun to settle early, even before they were married. Routine had been part of their protection against the outside world. Nevertheless there had been, at the beginning, no dearth of those sudden moments of desire. When had Saturday afternoons begun? She tried to remember, but could not. Too long ago, certainly well before she was pregnant, because they had been modified during the last weeks before Jonathan was born, when she had grown huge, needing the reassurance of being desired all the more, but with neither of them able to do much about it. Did Jeremy and his wife have a similar arrangement? Probably. Jeremy was so very organised.

'How long have you been married, Jeremy?'

'Two years.'

He was twenty-three, she knew. He must have started his landscape gardening business and got married at much the same time. That figured. He'd need someone to answer the telephone. 'You married young.'

'Not for round here. People in a village marry early or late, with not much in between, stands to reason.'

'What reason?'

'You grow up with people – girls you've known all your life. By the time you're both eighteen you could have been going together for five years, so you might as well get married. If not, you've missed the boat, and you have to take what you can get at thirty-five. My dad was married at eighteen. Betty and I waited until we were twenty-one, but that was because I had to finish at college.'

Sarah remembered old Mrs Potter, Jeremy's grandmother, stomping out of the butcher's shop. Something had been said to annoy her, and it wasn't clear what. Somewhere there was an old Mr Potter, the Darby to her Joan, but he was seldom seen about the village, being crippled from a stroke. 'And your grandfather?'

'Different. He was a farm labourer, married the boss's daughter. Takes longer.' He cleared his throat. 'Do you want me to cut the grass, or will Mr Arnott do it on Sunday? Needs cutting twice a week this time of year, strictly speaking, but I don't expect miracles.'

'Simon will cut it. Your time's too valuable.' The Potters had arrived in 1923. How old would Jeremy's grandfather have been in 1948? His birth would be recorded in the parish register, she supposed. The Inspector would have checked on all that.

Interesting that Jeremy had not suggested that Simon should cut the grass on Saturday. It was possible to become paranoid about what the village did or did not know.

They sat again under the monkey-puzzle tree, looking over the valley. Miss Hedges had refused to open her lips until they were alone. This had hurt Adrian's feelings. 'Madam's in one of her moods, I'm afraid. Been like it for days. You're wasting your time. You won't get anything out of her. You'd be better off visiting Ethel; she's the one in the window, keeps calling out all the time for her hearing-aid. It gets monotonous, but at least it's conversation.'

Sarah let the silence grow between and around them until it felt comfortable. Then she spoke. 'You blame yourself?'

'Yes.'

'You shouldn't.'

'That's for me to decide.'

'You blame me?'

'No.'

'I think you do.'

'You conclude incorrectly. Once I had pointed you in that direction, you were bound to follow your nose until you found her, if she were still alive to be found.'

'You wanted me to find her?'

'In a sense. I never wanted her death.'

'Why did you want me to find her?'

'Mischief. I'm old. We get bored. We become mischievous. We want to move the pieces.'

'You could have told the police about Doris Reeves. You didn't; you told me, and I told the police. You could have told the police about the Morris Eight, but you told me instead, and I kept it to myself, followed it through myself, made rather a mess of it if you want to know. I didn't intend her death either – God knows I didn't – never imagined for a moment, but . . . . If there's any blame, Miss Hedges, it has to fall on me.'

'You'd better read the letter.'

Her bag was in her lap, and she took from it an envelope with a blue second-class stamp, removed the letter, and handed it to Sarah.

Sarah read the letter, watched by Miss Hedges.

My dear Charis,

You will not be surprised to hear from me, even though so much time has passed unmarked by any communication between us since last we saw each other. I am deeply sorry to learn from Mrs Arnott that you have been admitted to the old folks' Home at Temple Glazeby, because I well know how harshly such a place would be bound to irk someone of your spirit. I would urge a Christian acceptance on you, but even now, as I write, I can see your face before me wearing its wicked look, and hear you say, "Don't try your tricks on me, Lily Partridge, for I am the heathen within your gates." Oh, Charis, those were good times! I have found Fellowship since, of course, and much fulfilment in parish work, both here and in James's previous pastorate, but I shall never forget the school at Radcote, and my happiness in working with the children, and your dear self among them.

Mrs Arnott came to me, as you must know, with questions about the past which disturbed me, and which I have to admit that I evaded to some extent. On reflection, I do not believe that she will be satisfied, and it seems that a matter long closed is now to be re-opened, with consequences which can only be painful to those concerned who are still alive, and harmful to the memories of those who may be dead. Consequently I have come to the decision that I do not choose to assist in such a re-opening, and I prefer instead to withdraw from it in the only way available to me.

I should like to have talked this over with some sympathetic person. There are questions of theology involved which I do not entirely fathom. No Christian has the right to take any life, even one's own; only God has the right to decide when the life He gave must end. That has always been my belief, and it still is. Yet He has given His children the gift of free will also, to choose between good and evil, and it cannot be good to cause unnecessary pain. Our Saviour is merciful; that I know. If my choice should be mistaken, He will respect the intention and intercede for me. To His goodness and mercy I commend my soul.

Do not grieve for me, Charis. Mrs Arnott will tell you what I have told her, that I do not fear death – any more than you must do, my dear. And for what comes after, I put my trust in God's infinite mercy, both for myself and, when your own time shall come, for my dear heathen within the gates who shall yet, by our Saviour's grace, be received into Eternal Life.

Until that time, my dear, remember me. I send my blessings and my love.

Your sincere friend,
Lily Partridge.

'You read the bit about eternal life?'

'Yes.'

'Fool! Idiot!' Miss Hedges wiped her nose with the back of her hand and blinked furiously.

'You can't know she's done it.'

'I do know.'

'It's only a letter. She may have changed her mind. She had to go out and post this after she'd written it. If she'd left it by her body or in the room somewhere, it wouldn't have been sent on to you; the police would have it.'

'I made it my busines to find out. It wasn't easy. One has no privacy here. But I had to be sure. I wrote to you first. You didn't come.'

'I'm here now.'

'I needed you at once. I knew nothing. I hadn't seen you since you came before, only a bloody parcel of books. But the letter told me you'd been to visit her, so you must know where she was. There was no address at the top, only the date, but the postmark was Penrith. Right! Help yourself, Hedges; nobody else will. I had to do what you must have done – ask Directory Enquiries – but I don't have my own phone, and we get no pocket-money here, none to speak of, because there's nothing to buy, certainly not enough for a long-distance phone call. I went to the Warden. Never mind our Saviour's infinite mercy; it was the bloody Warden I had to trust. Couldn't tell her everything, couldn't very well show her the letter, not with your name all over it. Said I'd heard from an old friend out of the blue, contemplating suicide and she hadn't given an address. The Warden let me use the phone in her office, went out and closed the door, left me to it. Good mark, that girl! Gold star! I found the number, phoned, and got some Welsh woman. Told me everything, couldn't stop talking. Lily took the bus into Wigton to collect some dry-cleaning. Called in at the health-food shop, bought some kind of herbal remedy – valerian, lettuce leaves or something: the Welsh bitch swore by it to promote sound sleep without troubling the doctor. Came home, everything normal, watched TV, cooked herself supper, then drank her bedtime cocoa, went to bed, took the bottleful of tablets, pulled the plastic cover from the dry-cleaning over her head, and they found her in the morning. Suffocated, but she'd been sick first, and then choked on the vomit.'

'"They" found her?'

'The woman. On the borrow, I expect. The Welsh usually are.'

'The woman helped her with the shopping – and in all sorts of ways, I think. She was a bit nosey, but she did seem concerned.'

'Don't ask me to be generous, Sarah Arnott. I have to attack somebody. Be glad it's not you.'

'I'm sorry. I know you're upset.'

'Valerian! Lettuce juice! She could have got Mogadon from the doctor, and done it properly at least. I think of her

. . . vomiting . . . choking . . . being sick . . . changing her mind, and struggling with the plastic.'

'The woman didn't say that.'

'I imagine it. She dares to write to me about Our Saviour's infinite bloody mercy! There was a time for that bugger to be merciful. He could have burst the bag, and let her live, but it was too much bloody trouble.'

'Did she leave a note? To say why she'd done it?'

'She wrote that letter, the one you hold in your hand, and will return to me, please, now that you have read it.' Sarah gave her the letter. Miss Hedges folded it carefully and put it away again in her bag, looking down throughout the operation so that the tears which filled her eyes might not easily be seen. 'She wrote to me. Her husband is dead. She has no family. To whom else would she write?'

'There was the Welsh woman – her landlady – Mrs Bowen-Davies. It was in her house. Lily might have wanted to apologise for giving trouble. And there were people came to see her, ex-parishioners; they came once a week for Christian Fellowship. She might have wanted to explain to them.'

'She wanted to explain to me. We were friends; we were young together, two of a kind in many ways, if you exclude religion. And I had sent you to her. She wanted me to know. The others would know anyway because they would find her; the woman would find her. I would never know, unless she told me, so she wrote a letter, and sent it second-class to give herself time.'

The tears were falling freely now, and Miss Hedges shook her head angrily to shake them away. Sarah said, 'I suppose the police will want to interview you. You'll have to receive them, I'm afraid. They'll want the letter.'

'No.'

'They may insist. The landlady will have told them about your phone call.'

'She doesn't know who I am, and where I was phoning from, anything about me. I never gave my name, and she was too busy talking to ask. When I knew what I needed to know, I hung up. She can tell them what she likes. There's no way of finding me.'

Sarah remained silent. There was a way, of course. She had concealed too much from the Inspector already. She wished she knew more about the law. To deny information to the police was a criminal act; it was considered to be abetting. But if they didn't ask, was one bound to tell? People in the Crime Club stories often kept silent or told direct lies in order to protect a lover or children or even a spouse, not that it ever did any good, and were seldom prosecuted for it. Miss Hedges said, 'There's no way the police can know unless you tell them, and you won't.'

'No.' It was true. She would not betray Miss Hedges. 'I shan't give up, though.'

'I haven't asked you to.'

'Never mind about war crimes, I want to know who killed Dorrie. When I know, I'll decide what to do.'

'Up to you.'

'I'll want to talk to you again when you feel better.'

'What did Lily say to you? About not fearing death?'

'She said she was frightened of senility, not death. She said she'd seen too much of it in her parish work. She said the old are often glad to die.'

'Well, she was right there. She was wrong-headed in a lot of ways, was Lily, and her husband more so, but she was right there.' The tears had dried on Miss Hedges's cheeks, and her chin came up again. 'Can you be sure I'll be here when you come again?'

'You're not the suicidal type. And anyway I don't imagine they make it easy here.'

'Nothing's impossible. I am more the Antique Roman then the Dane. We'll see. Wheel me in now.

We'll give Adrian the good news that I'm talking again. If that is good news.'

The Inspector arrived unannounced, bearing flowers and wearing an abashed expression. It seemed pointless to Sarah that he should bring gladioli to someone whose garden was already full of irises, but she accepted them with good grace and arranged them in a jug. Then she took him into the conservatory, where they sat drinking coffee with Jonathan in his chair between them, so that Sarah could easily divide her attention.

'You're bringing me back into the case?'

'Up to a point. If you will.'

'You want me to start asking questions again?'

'Only of Miss Hedges.'

'She's not very well at the moment. A friend of hers died suddenly in Cumbria, and it upset her.'

'Yes, I heard you'd been again.'

'Someone has to visit her.'

'I've had a bit of a problem with your Doris Reeves. It seems she doesn't exist.' Sarah's head turned sharply. She managed to bite back her immediate reply which would have been, 'Of course she exists. The vicar's wife remembered her,' but nothing much came out in its place except a rather squeaky 'Oh!'. Luckily the Inspector needed no positive encouragement to continue. 'Leastways she did exist, in the village at least, but nowhere else, and certainly not in Nottingham.'

'You've been to Nottingham?'

'I have been through channels. I've liaised with my colleagues in Nottingham. In 1948 there were Reeveses in Nottingham of course, several on the electoral register, both men and women, families and single persons; it's a common name. But no mother living apart from her husband with a daughter named Doris. Only one Doris Reeves at that time in the whole city, and she was in the Geriatric Ward of the local hospital.'

'Dental records? You did say you had a respect for dentists.'

'The dental records are for the old lady. In 1948, the National Health Service started. She took advantage of it with a complete set of brand new choppers.'

'DHSS? National Insurance Number?'

'Doris would have been issued with a card at the age of sixteen when she left school. The address on the card would have been her address at that time, presumably her home – wherever that was. I don't know, Mrs Arnott, how many Doris Reeveses, countrywide, left school in – when would it have been – 1942? 43 – during the war anyway. Those records don't exist any more. Thereafter, back in the days just after the war, wherever she went – job, further education, whatever – a new card was issued every year, to be completed by the employed person. Our young lady could have put any address she chose on it. That might have been Nottingham, it might have been her lodgings in the village, it might have been anywhere; nobody would have checked up, and anyway those records are not kept for fifty years. If we had her National Insurance number, of course we'd be able to trace her under any name she chose to adopt, but we don't'.

'The County Education Department payment records would have it.'

'The payment records aren't kept, and her application form for a job at the school was destroyed four years after she left. We forget, Mrs Arnott: they didn't have microfiches, and they didn't keep useless pieces of paper.'

'Teacher training college?'

'Which? We don't know what name she would have given, and we can't even know that she went to one, that she had any qualifications at all. She was only a supply teacher, and a village church school would have had to take what it could get in those days.'

'But Miss Hedges gave her the job, and might remember. That's what you want me to ask?'

'If you would be so good.'

'You said she did exist as far as the village was concerned. You've asked about? People remember the schoolmistress?'

'Right! Application form . . . pay-slips . . . gone! But you ask village people who were children at the school in forty-seven and forty-eight, and they remember Miss Reeves. Look in the school log book – those books go back to 1863 – and there she is, sure enough. Billy Garbett and his sister get stuck up to their chests in snow on your hill, and Miss Reeves goes out and finds them. Fascinating stuff, a kind of social history, you could say, though a bit vague on detail for my purposes. Still, she's in the book: Miss Reeves is there. Nothing that would let you identify her in any legal way, nothing to prove she really is Miss Reeves, but someone who called herself Miss Reeves did teach at that school.'

'Snapshots. Photos. School picture.' Jonathan caught the excitement and joined in, making approving noises and waving his fists in front of him.

'Your lad all right?'

'You're not a family man.'

'Never saw much of mine at this age.'

'He's all right. Just getting in on the act, that's all. School picture.'

'There is one.'

'You can make an identifiction, then. Reconstruct the face from the skeleton. I was reading about it a few months ago in the Sunday papers. Some builders found the skeleton of a teenage girl wrapped in carpet in a back yard in . . . I can't remember where . . . Cardiff or somewhere. Anyway, the Forensic people got to work and produced a

Photofit. Bingo! Your problem's solved. No need for me to harry Miss Hedges.'

He was looking at her. He had that patient look her mother sometimes wore. 'Mrs Arnott, have you any idea how much that would cost?'

'It's a murder enquiry.'

'It's forty-two years old. I say to you again what I've had occasion to say before. Any guilty party has to be either over sixty or dead. I wish to solve this crime because it is my training to solve any crime – any major crime – but I cannot sanction that kind of expense. Now, please!' He drained his mug and stood up. 'Oblige me! When next you visit Miss Hedges – which I hope may be sooner rather than later – if you could just find out for me what qualifications this girl had, whether she'd been trained and if so where, schooling, letters of reference, anything she can remember that would assist me to know who the girl calling herself Doris Reeves really was.'

Sarah said, 'I think she was Doris Reeves.' Dorrie had appeared in her dreams, not the Inspector's. If she was really somebody else, she would have said so.

It was no good; she would never change. All her life she would go on blundering into situations unprepared, improvising, not really knowing what she wanted or how to get it even if she did know. She never made lists. She never wrote 'Pro' and 'Con' on the right and left sides of a sheet of paper with a line between. She never analysed a problem, anticipating the probable reactions to her own action and sketching out further courses of action in response to each reaction. She could not play chess, and her experiences with backgammon, gin rummy and even halma had been unhappy.

What did she want from Dorrie's Morris Eight? She had wanted to know if Mrs Partridge had told the truth and the car was still to be found at the bottom of the vicarage garden. But she already knew that it was: Jeremy had said so. So what did she hope to gain by going to see for herself? Did she really imagine that, after forty-eight years, the car itself would tell her something? Yes, she hoped the car would tell her something.

What was she to say to the media people who lived at the vicarage now? Should she suggest, as she had to Jeremy, that her husband was interested in restoring the car? No, because they would expect Simon to come with her, and he would probably refuse, and even if he were to come, he was a mechanical ignoramus, so the media people would know at once that they were lying. There! that was planning: she had anticipated a reaction and two possible consequences, both, as it happened, adverse. Right! She was capable of change; anyone can change. She set out towards Simon's study to get a notebook in which to sketch out a plan, but put the kettle on first for coffee and then remembered that the bed was still unmade and there were damp towels on the bathroom floor and Jonathan would be awake by eleven. Half an hour later, with the bedroom and bathroom tidied, Jonathan awake and fed and shopping to be done in the village, she realised that she still had not worked out what to say to the media people.

Well, one didn't need to make plans in a notebook for that; it wasn't difficult. She would ask to look at their garden; she would say that Jeremy had praised it. People were always glad to show off their gardens. And if the media people weren't at home, she would go in anyway, and apologise later.

'Ant! Somebody wants to look at the garden.'

The female media person was the colour of well-seasoned elm, with straight hair bleached blonde and falling to her shoulders, and very white teeth. She was wearing rompers and an expression of barely controlled panic, which Sarah considered to be an over-reaction to her own polite and reasonable request, but it was possible that near-panic was the customary response of any media person to the unexpected, and one must think nothing of it. The rompers were easily explained. Sarah had seen them illustrated in the fashion pages of a Sunday colour supplement earlier in the year.

'I could wander round by myself if you like. I'm quite respectable. Anyone in he village will vouch for me.'

Ant appeared from an inner room. He seemed to be older than his wife, or else he had taken less care of himself. He was snorting into an enormous handkerchief and wore what Sarah took to be some kind of uniform – tinted spectacles, jeans and trainers, and a T-shirt with the words 'Kindness Can Kill' printed across the front. His beard ran all the way round his chin then up into his sideburns, on over his ears and ended in a scruffy patch of hair like a rabbit's scut at the back of his head. Small patches of it seemed to have been pulled out, but that may merely have been an idiosyncratic form of alopecia brought on by stress. The top of his head was totally bald but mottled with brown spots, and shone like well-waxed furniture. His eyes and nose were moist and red with hayfever. 'She's collecting for something,' he said. 'Gypsy. Bound to be. Look at the pram. That child won't be hers,' and went back into his sanctum.

'We live on the hill. You can see our house from your back door.'

'Don't take any notice of him; he's in the throes. And it's the worst time of year, you know. The garden's no pleasure. We should be by the sea or on some Greek island, but *que sera, sera*.' Maybe the woman's expression was not panic at all but the result of an injudicious eye make-up combined with an open mouth and cerise lipstick. Their name was Bazely, Ant and Wendy. She did the interviews,

Sarah had been told; her husband wrote and produced – if he really was her husband: the village was not convinced, since letters came for her under a different name, which she also sometimes used to sign cheques. 'Are you sure you want to look at the garden? It's not much to do with us, you know; we can't claim any credit for it. We can't even sit out in it at the moment, with the pollen count what it is. Jeremy Potter looks after it.'

'He looks after ours as well.'

'What a dish!' the woman said gloomily. 'Doesn't it make you sick?' And Sarah could see, having now had the time to study her, that the woman was considerably older than her appearance at first suggested, far older than was customary for a television interviewer, which might be why she and Ant had been relegated to a local interest programme.

So they made a tour of the garden, leaving Jonathan in his pram under a tree, and there at the far end of it, almost entirely hidden by clematis montana, was the Morris Eight. 'That's interesting,' Sarah said, 'how did you manage to get it in there?'

'Nothing to do with us; it was there when we came. We just grew the clematis over it. I wanted to get rid of it, sell it for scrap, pay someone to tow it away even, but Jeremy said it was a feature, so we kept it.'

'Jeremy said?'

'You know what he is. You can't argue with him. It was just the same about the pampas grass.'

'Looks like a vintage car,' Sarah said. 'It might be worth something.'

She looked back towards the pram to check on Jonathan's wellbeing. Ant was watching them from a window. When he saw her looking at him, he turned away and pretended to clean his spectacles. Wendy said, 'He won't settle as long as you're here, and he won't come out and be neighbourly either. I despair of him sometimes. I mean, for Christ's sake, everybody's insecure. Let's go into Fingal's Cave and take a good look at the car. Do you really think it's worth anything? We could do with the money at the moment.'

They parted the curtain of clematis and went in. The car had been parked in a corner, just clear of the garden wall, close to what might once have been a compost heap into which the clematis had been planted and from which it arched profusely over the car, forming a grotto in which nothing grew. Sarah had thought that a Morris Eight would resemble the beetle-shaped Morris Minors which may still be seen on country roads, driven at forty miles an hour by some senior citizen with a tail of cars behind hooting and flashing their lights, but in fact it did look far more like one of those vintage cars in which Dorrie had driven the unhappy hotel manager to Brighton, with a body like a biscuit tin and running boards.

She had expected to find a disintegrating construction of rusty metal, but only the running boards had rusted where the rubber had perished and fallen away, leaving a jagged edge on which the schoolkid of whom Jeremy had spoken must have cut his leg. The rest of the bodywork had been protected by its paint, which had faded and cracked but still seemed to be intact and not to have been much affected by the thick deposit of bird droppings on the roof and bonnet. The laminated glass of the windscreen had gone yellow, and the chrome of the door handles and around the headlamps had corroded. Sarah thought of Doris Reeves's skeleton, the bones clean, and the clean bones of the foetus inside the pelvis. Dorrie's car had decayed more slowly than its owner: the trimmings were still in place. 'Shall we see if the door opens?' she said.

What are you looking for, Sarah Arnott, what do you expect to find? So far the car had told her nothing except that there was a discrepancy between the testimonies of Jeremy Potter and Wendy Bazely as to which of them was responsible for its continued presence at the bottom of the vicarage garden. The grotto was not accidental. Wires had been strung above the roof of the car, forming a framework by which the clematis had climbed. Only Jeremy could have done that; the Bazelys were not gardeners. And Jeremy would know that, among the whole clematis family, only a montana would grow so grossly. Had his intention been to conceal the Morris Eight as an eyesore or to protect it? And as for the Bazelys, though their presence in the Midlands (instead of on a Greek island) may have been because they had to go where they could get work, why, considering Ant's hayfever, had they made their home in a country vicarage, with every breeze an aerosol of pollen, when they might have rented a high-rise flat in Birmingham?

She reached out to the door handle. The weatherproof strips around the glass of the windows had absorbed moisture and had grown moss. The handle turned and the door opened easily: the hinges had not rusted. The leather upholstery was mouldy and smelled of damp. There was more moss growing on the carpets inside. The padding of the interior roof was mildewed and sagging, with the stitches rotted away: it fell six inches as the door opened. She put her hand inside, and the rotting fabric tore in strips. Nothing. Nothing in the glove compartment, nothing tucked above the sun visors, nothing in the side pockets, nothing pushed down between or beneath the seats. 'What are you looking for?' said Wendy Bazely.

'I'm so sorry. Treasure. Ever since I was a kid, I've been fascinated by anything – you know? – abandoned – junk – old trunks – stuff you find in attics: I'd spend hours looking. I was always sure I'd find money . . . a ring . . . bracelets . . . buttons . . . some forgotten valuables. You've really touched on my secret vice with this car. I do apologise. It's very rude.'

'That's okay. Feel free. Want to open the bonnet? If

there's a diamond pendant tucked into the ignition system, we'll go halves.'

The bonnet opened sideways and with some difficulty. The two women opened it together, Sarah feeling foolish. Nothing. The fan belt had rotted, and so had all the insulation, and whether the engine, by whatever miracle of restoration, could be made to work or not was beyond Sarah. 'I thought it was the car might be valuable,' Wendy said. 'As an antique.'

'I don't know how many may have survived. I think they were rather common.'

'You don't surprise me.'

Sarah stood back as far as the tendrils of clematis would allow, and looked at the Morris Eight. It continued to tell her nothing. Thirty-six pounds! Had it really been an act of disguised charity, far more than the car was worth? One could get more than that for one of the wheels today. They were spoke-wheels, such as are still seen on customised cars, and seemed to be in good condition, though the rubber tyres had perished. The spare wheel, strapped to the back and resting in a sort of trough specially constructed to receive it, was particularly handsome. 'I suppose you could get something for the wheels,' she said.

'Do you think so?' Genuine delight, whatever that might signify.

'Look at that spare, It's a collectors' item.' She put her hand on the wheel, and gripped it; she had learned nothing from her experience with the fabric of the interior roof. The perished rubber of the tyre, the rotted leather of the strap, could no longer hold the wheel in place, and it toppled over.

'What do you think you're doing with the car?' Ant had left the house, unnoticed, and was watching her from the other side of the curtain of clematis.

'She thinks the wheels may be worth something.'

'Deals in them, does she?'

Sarah said, 'No. Just a guess. I could easily be wrong.' There was something written in the trough, letters or signs of some sort scratched into the paintwork. She wished very strongly that Wendy and Ant would go away and leave her alone with the Morris Eight, now that it had decided to break its silence. She was at the wrong angle and too far away to see exactly what the scratching was, though she could tell that there was a cross at the top. Ant's eyes were red from the hayfever, and his stare intense. He seemed to be trying to hold her with his gaze so as to prevent her getting a better look. Well, she would not be held. She moved a little, casually, glancing down, and broke the contact. Yes, it was certainly a cross, and no, the Bazelys were not going to go away.

She had not been casual enough. Wendy had noticed the direction of her glance, and moved to look at the writing, pushing the spare wheel out of the way, so that, collectors' item or not, it fell unregarded to the ground.

'It's Latin.'

'May I see?'

Ant sneezed, and in doing so broke the power of his gaze, freeing Sarah. He put out his hands towards the clematis; if he were to regain control, he must join the women in the grotto. But the tendrils of clematis were studded with seed-heads. If Art were to push them aside, the seed-heads would brush against his face. Hundreds of seeds, held on tiny cilia, would lodge in his beard: he would erupt with eczema. Ant turned, and ran back across the lawn, head down.

It was certainly a cross, set as on a tombstone, at the top of an inscription which had been scratched deep into the paintwork with a pointed metal implement, perhaps a bradawl. Beneath the cross were the initials 'DR', and then the words, '*REQUIESCE IN PACE*', and below that more words in Latin, '*DEUS DONUM PRETIOSUM EI DEDIT, ET ILLA AD FORUM ID TULIT*.'

The two women puzzled together over the inscription. Sarah wondered how long it had been since she had shared an intellectual occupation of any sort with another woman. Too long. Wendy said, 'Can you make it out?'

'I can make out the words. I'm not sure about the meaning. *Deus* is God, of course. *Donum* might be something like "donation" –gift. The Forum was where Mark Antony made that speech. *Requiesce in pace*? That's interesting.'

'His chisel must have slipped. It should be *at*, shouldn't it?'

'Maybe.'

'It's what they put on gravestones, isn't it? Used to put, before there was cremation. "RIP" "*Requiescat in pace*". "Rest in peace".'

'That's the interesting bit. *Requiescat* doesn't mean "Rest"; it means "He rests" or "She rests". That's why it's on gravestones. You know? – after life's fitful fever, she sleeps well.' Sarah could feel her mother stirring within her like the coils of a snake, but she did not care: she was sharing insights. 'But this isn't *requiescat*, it's *requiesce*: that's the second person singular, I think, like "*tu*" in French, the one you use to children or lovers or people you don't rate: it's not the polite form.' Wendy's mouth was open again, but in admiration, not panic. Sarah began positively to like her. 'So it might be a command, "Rest in peace", meaning "Don't come back and haunt me." And he's talking to someone he didn't like, or else he liked too much. Or both. Interesting!'

'"He"?'

'Whoever. You said "his chisel" yourself. Could be she: it doesn't take much to scratch in paint. If you don't mind, I'll just get my notebook from the pram.'

ARSON

Simon took the Latin to town with him. The advertising agency with which his department worked had an unfrocked priest on the staff as Religious Consultant. He should be able to translate the inscription, and might know also whether it were a quotation, and if so, from what. Both the words themselves and the source from which they had been taken might provide insight. Meanwhile Sarah fretted.

Dorrie had bought the car secondhand, so the possibility that the inscription under the spare wheel might have been already there when she bought it had to be considered. Sarah considered it for about five seconds, and then rejected it. 'DR' – 'Doris Reeves', then a cross, followed by a sentence in Latin, beginning with the word '*Deus*'; it had to be an epitaph. Therefore the inscription was made after Dorrie was dead, therefore by someone who knew she was dead, therefore maybe by the someone who had killed her, and this someone had easy access to her car and knew enough Latin to write an epitaph. The figure of James Elroy Partridge, vicar of the parish of Radcote from 1940 to 1953, began to thicken up in Sarah's deductive mind. Was this the reason Mrs Partridge had committed suicide? James Elroy was now deceased, safe from arrest as the Inspector had surmised the murderer might by now be, and it seemed a little excessive for his widow to kill herself merely to protect his good name, but she had, Sarah remembered, said something to that effect in her letter to Miss Hedges, something about an investigation being harmful to the memories of those who were dead.

It was so immediately satisfying as to be unsatisfying. No Crime Club detective would buy it; it was too neat. Why should the vicar kill her?

These people who were alive before one was born! How was one to understand them? Nobody was allowed to teach in a school these days, even a primary school, without some sort of qualification. But back in 1948, the Inspector had said, a village school would have had to take what it could get. Who was Doris Reeves? Where had she come from? Forged references? Sarah did not believe that someone with forged references, pretending to be a teacher, would have fooled Miss Hedges, or not for long, even though Miss Hedges had been younger then. (How young? She was in her eighties now. Therefore in her early forties. No, she would not have been fooled by any blatant impostor.) What – or who – had there been in Radcote to cause Dorrie, an outsider, ostensibly from Nottingham, to apply for a job at the school? That was the key. Someone or something about the village had attracted Dorrie to it, and after two years, when Dorrie was pregnant, maybe as a consequence of that attraction, she had been murdered there.

Wait! Wait! This was going too fast. Something about the village had attracted Sarah and Simon. They had found a barn there – or just outside – up for conversion, at a price they could afford and with a magnificent view; it didn't follow, or Sarah certainly hoped it didn't, that they would be murdered in consequence. Doris Reeves, for whatever reason, had wanted a job as a supply teacher in a village school, and there had been one going at Radcote. The rest was all guesswork.

Simon returned from London with the translation. 'It's

dog Latin. "God gave her a precious gift, and she took it to the marketplace." Means she was putting it about, I suppose.'

'Whoring?'

'What else?'

'In the village?'

'Presumably.'

'That's ridicuous.' Sarah found herself growing angry. This was not her vision of Dorrie at all. 'You don't suggest she stood at street corners? Sidled up to customers at the pub? Everybody knew her. She lodged with the vicar and his wife. They were on friendly terms. It wasn't the kind of place she could bring someone back to.'

'I don't suggest anything. I'm just telling you what it says. She took her precious gift to the marketplace – has to mean she was on the game. Father Curtis thought the same.'

'I thought you said he'd been defrocked.'

'They still call him "Father" at the agency. Look, Sarah, she didn't have to stand at street corners or take punters back to her room at the vicarage. Discreet visiting. Local farmers. Back seat of a car in a lay-by. Frolics in a haybarn. She could build up a connection. It probably still goes on, that kind of thing.'

'How do you know what goes on? You're never here.'

'I don't know why you're in such a rage. I get you the information you want, and you snap at me. You're so scratchy these days; I never know what I'm coming home to. You could be giving me a grateful hug; you could be pouring me a gin and tonic; you could be saying, "Thank you, Simon, for going to so much trouble." Instead – '

'All right! Thank you, Simon. I'll get you a gin and tonic.'

'It all happened a long time ago, love. It's really not important.'

'It's important to me. You look after Jonathan, and I'll get your drink.'

Simon picked Jonathan up, and jiggled him up and down, to his delight, talking to him seriously in baby-talk. 'Wigga wigga wuncle! Who's a great carbuncle?' and, calling to Sarah in the kitchen, 'Do I dare to tell you he needs changing?'

'So what else is new?' She returned with the gin and tonic, took Jonathan and set him squashily back in his chair. 'What's dog Latin?'

'I asked Father Curtis that. He says it's the kind of Latin a schoolboy might write, or some hick Irish priest who wasn't comfy with the Litany.' Jonathan set up a howl. 'I'll change him if you'll just let me take a sip of this nourishing nectar first.'

As Sarah had once told her mother during one of their arguments, Simon, when he was home and when he chose, was often a good father to Jonathan, changing him sometimes, cuddling him when he cried, playing with him and talking to him as all the books recommended.

'Right!' Sarah's mother had said. 'Every time the telephone rings, Jonathan says "Dadda".' Sarah's mother's insistence on facing reality was seldom comfortable or intended to be. She had managed in one sentence to remind her daughter, first that Simon would always put his family second to his job, second that the telephone didn't actually ring all that often.

No better than she should be? Did it mean that? It was so naff if that was all the inscription meant. If Dorrie was putting it about, the father could have been anybody. One was not murdered for putting it about, except by a serial killer who had a thing about prostitutes, in which case he would not have bothered to bury the body and there would have been a lot of others littering the fields and hedgerows.

Classically, unmarried pregnant women were murdered by those who had impregnated them and who would otherwise have been blackmailed into marrying or at least maintaining them.

'Putting it about': it was naff, and it led nowhere. Also, if it were common knowledge – as in a village it would soon get to be, even under Simon's scenario of haybarn and lay-by – that Dorrie was putting it about, there would have been complaints at the school, deputations of outraged mothers, anonymous letters to Miss Hedges and the County Education Authority. She was only a supply techer, hired from term to term; she would not have been asked back.

What if she had been putting it about to just one person, getting paid but by a steady client? That one person would have been the father and would not have wished his parenthood to be made public, but – big but – why should he have scratched the epitaph on the car? There was a possibility that the person who killed Dorrie and the one who wrote the epitaph were not the same, though the epitaph-maker knew what had been going on, knew that Dorrie had put her precious gift on the open market, knew how she had died, whether by accident, sickness or murder, knew who had buried her body, but had for some reason kept the secret. Back came James Elroy Partridge into the picture, but not so solidly, because although one could imagine the vicar's keeping quiet about a murder during the 1940s before the death penalty had been abolished, if he believed there were extenuating circumstances, surely if he had known that Dorrie was putting it about, he would have turned her out of the vicarage? The Church of England was not as liberal in 1948 as it has since, in certain dioceses, become.

There was, of course, another reason for murdering a woman who had been putting it about, and that was jealousy. If some innocent unwordly person, or maybe some childhood sweetheart from wherever the elusive Miss Reeves had spent her childhood, had believed himself to be the father of Dorrie's unborn child and had then discovered that she was putting it about in Radcote and adjacent villages, he might have killed her in a jealous rage and written the epitaph also. But why on the car in the vicarage garden? – unless he lived in the vicarage. Was James Elroy Partridge beginning to firm up a little? Clergymen used to be thought unworldly, but, living in the village, and visiting his parishioners daily, James Elroy must have heard any gossip, and if there was none, if Dorrie's discretion had been absolute and nobody knew, then he would not have known either. No, better to leave James Elroy on one side for the moment. He had to remain a possible adulterer, a possible murderer, and maybe his widow had been protecting his good name by her suicide, but if that were so, with both of them dead there didn't seem to be anywhere for the investigation to go. It was still too neat, and there were other possibilities. (She could hear her mother in her head, remarking that the reason Sarah was so ready to put the Reverend J.E. Partridge on one side might be that it was not much fun to hunt a prey already dead.)

She had promised the Inspector that she would question Miss Hedges about Dorrie, and promised Miss Hedges to come and see her again, and might keep both promises with one visit, which she now much wanted to make, but it would have to wait until Wednesday because Jonathan could not be left. How did other mothers manage? Their own mothers helped out, of course, and sisters, old schoolfriends, close neighbours, women with whom they had attended the ante-natal clinic and who had since become buddies until persistent chat about their babies' progress began to pall. Creches: they used creches; there were nappy creches for babies under eighteen months and non-nappy creches for those over. Sarah had access to none of those. She loved her baby, she was besotted with him, but there were times when she grew very tired of being tied to him, physically tied, as if the umbilical cord had never been cut.

If Dorrie had been putting it about, would the children at the school have known? Schoolchildren always do know more about their teachers than the teachers know is known. Villagers who had been pupils at the school when Miss Reeves was teaching would be in their late forties or early fifties now. It was an area of enquiry Sarah had neglected, though the Inspector had not, but the Inspector did not know what she knew and might not have asked the right questions. He had established that Dorrie had existed and was remembered by those she had taught; he had said there was a school photograph. And he had questioned (or she supposed he had) men who might have been the father of her child and other villagers who had known these men, but had he asked Dorrie's own pupils about her way of life? If she had not been putting it about, at least not overtly, so that it was not a matter of common gossip, there might be aspects of Dorrie's character and behaviour which only the children knew.

Forty-two years – would they remember? One did remember odd things. Sarah could remember that Mrs Parrish, who had taught her History, always smelled of honey-and-lemon face-cream, and used to stroke the right side of her cheek, where she had a small birthmark. Odd things were what Sarah wished to know about Dorrie, odd things which would lie about like pieces of a jigsaw and then magically come together in her mind. She wished that the Inspector had shown her the school photograph in which Dorrie appeared, but he shared nothing with her which he did not wish to share, since he did not regard her, except when it suited him, as a partner in the investigation.

If Dorrie really had been putting it about or had been

untruthfully said to have been doing so – another possibility to be considered – then the Inspector would know that by now, and had not shared that knowledge either. Could he be persuaded to share? Crime Club detectives often worked in tandem with the police, the detective being, of course, the senior partner and the policeman the admiring foil. Because she was a woman, the Inspector might find such a partnership demeaning, but Sarah would not hog the superior position; they would collaborate as equals. If, for instance, Sarah were to tell him about the epitaph, it would complement or contradict evidence he already had. Either would be valuable. Together they could discuss the light each shed on the other. Since he had warned her that it would be dangerous for her to question the villagers, Sarah would happily leave him to ask any further questions, provided that they shared the answers. So they would go on.

It occurred to Sarah that she herself had not been forward in the matter of sharing. She had kept the epitaph to herself, together with the whole business of the sale of the car, her own visit to Cumbria, and Lily Partridge's suicide. If she were to start sharing now, it would all have to come spilling out, which would be horribly embarrassing and get the partnership off to a bad start. It was the Inspector's own fault, of course; she would never have kept information from him if he had not told her to drop out of the investigation. But would he realise that?

It came to her that there was no need to wait until Wednesday before talking to Miss Hedges. The old folks' Home at Temple Glazeby was not a prison, but more like a boarding school for girls – old girls in this case. If Miss Hedges's wheelchair could be collapsed, like Jonathan's pram, she was transportable and might be invited out to tea. Sarah telephoned at once and was told that Miss Hedges was in bed with a temperature; there was a virus going round the Home, thought to have been brought in by the window-cleaners. There was no reason why she should not be taken out for the afternoon as soon as she was well, but no telling when that would be.

That night there was a fire in the vicarage garden. Sarah, who had been finding it difficult to get to sleep lately, woke suddenly to the sound of Jonathan at full bellow; it was possible that his first teeth were really beginning to come through. Simon groaned, and put a pillow over his head, so Sarah got out of bed, picked Jonathan out of his cot, and, since it would have been both heartless and pointless to try to quieten him in the bedroom where Simon was still trying to sleep, took him downstairs. The living-room curtains were open, and there was enough moonlight for her to be able to walk about, rocking him and crooning.

As his howls began to subside into a grumble, she took him over to the window and looked out across the valley. There was a light in the village, not one of the streetlights, which were switched off at midnight anyway, but much larger. She opened the front door and went out onto the patio, then onto the drive. It was a warm still September night. Jonathan, catching her mood as he so often did, was quiet but wide awake. She moved down the drive and stood at the top of the rockery, staring at the light.

Simon joined her. 'Heard you open the front door. Brought your dressing-gown.' He slipped it over her shoulders.

'Something's happening in the village.'

'Looks like a bonfire got out of control.'

But it was not yet the season for bonfires, even if anyone were likely to make one in the middle of the night. The only time they had seen anything comparable down in the village was Guy Fawkes Night, when the communal village bonfire would be twice the height of a man, the wood augmented with rubber tyres, and that would be lighted early in the evening and be smouldering ashes by midnight.

Around the light of the fire other points of light had appeared, but these were only the lighted windows of village people, curious to know what was happening.

'Jonathan okay?'

'It's not cold.'

They stood together at the top of the rockery, and watched the local fire engine and a police car, blue lights flashing, career along the valley road. Though they were a mile away, the sirens could be clearly heard. By some acoustical quirk, sound came up clearly from the village to Garbett's Barn, usually the chimes of the ice-cream van on Saturday afternoons in summer.

'Hell of a blaze! Wonder what it is.'

But Sarah knew what it was. 'Come on, we'd better go in,' she said. 'He's quiet now.' She also knew that if someone still alive had set fire to Dorrie's car in the vicarage garden so as to destroy the epitaph, then the two Partridges could probably be crossed off the list of those who might have murdered her.

In the morning, the telephone rang. Wendy was tearful. She did not know how it could have happened. Vandals were spoken of: there had been a disco at the Village Hall which had not broken up until past midnight. Usually vandalism in the village did not extend beyond damage to the phone box, but this, the local policeman had told her, was technically breaking and entering and on a par with the occasion three years ago, when a back window at the pub had been broken and three bottles of vodka stolen, together with a quantity of cigarettes.

Sarah could hear guilt beneath the tears. She had better have it out of Wendy before it was buried too deep. She loaded Jonathan and his pushchair into the car and drove down to the vicarage to inspect the damage.

They looked together at the grotto which had once

housed and hidden the Morris Eight. The clematis had been totally burned away, together with most of what once had been a compost heap. The garden walls were blackened, the grass at the edge of the lawn burned, neighbouring shrubs singed, but the damage to the garden itself did not seem to be extensive. As for the car, it was now a shell. The perished rubber of the tyres had burned, leaving only the reinforcing wires as a tangle round the buckled rim and spokes of the wheels. The mildewed leather upholstery of the seats and the horsehair stuffing beneath had burned, so that the seats had become sets of springs in metal frames. The bakelite finish around the steering-wheel had burned, and the fire had melted and expanded the laminate in the glass of the windows, which had shattered and fallen out. The mossy carpet, the shredded fabric of the inside roof, all that had been destroyed, but the metalwork still held together. When one considered it, there had been surprisingly little of the car which was flammable, yet the fire had been visible for miles.

'I don't understand how it made such a big blaze. You had the fire engine, and everything.'

'They filled it with wood – old bits of fencing from the playing field, seed-trays from the shed, anything they could find. Then they piled the garden furniture around it – the deckchairs, the recliner with the canopy, the bench, picnic table, everything. They even took the back gate off its hinges.' And it was true, Sarah noticed; the little wooden gate leading out into Vicarage Lane was now a hole. 'They poured creosote over it – no, not creosote, that non-toxic stuff you're supposed to use for wood nowadays – and then petrol from the can we keep for the lawn-mower. They laid a trail of petrol back to the road.' A line of blackened grass led to the hole where the gate had been. 'Then they set it alight.'

'And you heard none of this?'

'It's a difficult time, what with all the cuts. No television programme's safe these days, however insignificant. God knows we're cheap enough, but even so . . . Ant and I haven't been sleeping very well recently.'

'Then you did hear? You were afraid to go out? I can understand that. Did you watch from the window?'

Wendy shook her head. 'Zonked. I don't really approve of pills, but it couldn't go on – lying awake, trying to get comfortable, breathing exercises, thinking about bloody waterlilies: you can go so far with bio-feedback, and then you crack.'

Sarah remembered Ant staring at them through the curtain of clematis. 'Both of you zonked?'

'Ant takes antihistamine tablets for his hayfever. They make him drowsy anyway.'

Was that an answer? Sarah though not. But it would be unwise to push any further on that front. There was still the question of the guilt she had sensed during Wendy's phone call. She looked again at the blackened metal of the Morris Eight. Essentially it was still all there. She had seen the blaze from the rockery, and imagined the whole thing burning, nothing left but ashes. But paintwork, upholstery, perished rubber, *they* burned; metal did not burn. The epitaph had been scratched through the paint into the metal. It must, under the soot, still be there.

In which case, why bother to burn the car?

Something was wrong with the metal trough which had held the spare wheel. It seemed to have changed its shape and swollen like the Elephant Man.

'What's that?'

'We had a little lead cupid. We bought it at a discount in a National Trust sale; I don't think Jeremy approved.' Wendy looked away. This was the guilt, part of the guilt, working up to it. 'We kept it on a plinth by the outdoor tomatoes. It was a joke – love-apples, you see. Tomatoes used to be called – '

'I know.'

'They piled it up with the other garden furniture. They couldn't have imagined it would burn.'

'It melted.'

'I'm afraid it's covered . . . .' It was like the vicar's wife all over again. Wendy's hands began washing each other. 'I don't know why they thought . . . .'

'I think we do know why.' Jonathan, who had been quiet so far, began to grizzle, and had to be picked up. Still catching moods! Sarah decided that she could do without the almost telepathic bond between mother and child; it only seemed to work one way.

'It was vandals; the village bobby said so. It could have happened any time. The disco's supposed to be teetotal, but he says they bring their own.'

'You told someone. Who?'

A mutinous pursing of the lips. 'You should have warned me. Whatever that Latin was, whatever it meant, you never said a word, but that was what you were looking for, wasn't it, when you came, pretending you just wanted to see the garden?'

'I didn't know what I was looking for.'

'It was that car, something to do with the car; I could tell by the way you. . . . And then we found the Latin, and you copied it into your book. Why did you bring a notebook if you didn't expect to find something?'

'I did expect to find something. Hoped to.'

'You should have confided in me. Trusted me. I can keep a secret.'

'But you didn't?'

'You never asked me to.'

'I'm not blaming you. Whom did you tell? Besides Ant? Where is Ant, by the way?'

'Gone to the studios. There's nothing to do there, but he can't bear disruption.'

'How much did you tell him?'

'Just that we'd found a Latin inscription on the car. He

went down and took a look at it – put a scarf over his face, and I held the clematis back, and he stared at it for a bit, but Ant doesn't understand Latin. I don't think he'll have connected it with the vandals. He didn't say anything about it this morning.'

'Just went off in a hurry and left you to talk to the policeman?'

'I don't know what you're suggesting.'

'Doesn't matter. Who else did you tell besides Ant?'

'The garage people. Gary and that retired man who works for him part-time. You'd said you thought those spoke-wheels might be valuable. I wanted to know what sort of dealer would buy them –whether there might be anyone in Leamington who went in for that kind of thing. I brought Gary back here and showed him the car. Of course he noticed the writing when he was looking at the spare wheel.'

'Did he notice it or did you point it out?'

'It was something to talk about.'

'Yes, I bet it was.' It would have been something to talk about all round the village, in the pub first if Gary were doing the talking, then in various homes, in the Spar, in the Post Office. 'And did you tell him my connection with it?'

'I told him you'd written it down.'

'And then vandals set fire to the car. And put a lead statue right on top of that trough so that it melted and covered up the writing.'

'We could try to get it off. Lead's quite soft. It ought to be easy to shift.'

'We will. But I think we'll discover that the writing's gone anyway.'

Wendy said, 'What did it mean, that Latin?' Sarah told her. 'Sounds as if she was on the game.'

'Maybe that's what we're meant to think, but I'm not sure I believe it. I'd like to talk to someone who knew her, but that might be more difficult now. Oh, shit! shit!' Jonathan's grizzle had turned into unmistakeable bad temper, and Sarah put him back in his pushchair. 'Have you got a banana I could mash or some fruit juice?'

'I'll look.' As they moved towards the kitchen Wendy said, 'I suppose it can't have been vandals, can it really? Not with putting that statue there? It's too much of a coincidence.'

'Right! If it had been you and Ant getting up their noses for some reason, they'd have wrecked the garden, broken your windows, scattered your garbage, set fire to the toolshed, not that car which was here before you came. No, it's someone – maybe more than one someone – who didn't know about that epitaph, or if he did know he didn't care because it was all hidden away and nobody was going to find it. But then you and I did find it, and I wrote the words in my notebook. So we both know about it, and we know what it says even though he's destroyed the original. And he knows we know. All the village knows by now – not what the epitaph says because it was in Latin, and you couldn't translate it for Gary, and he won't remember the words to repeat them – but they know we found it and that I copied it.'

'All the village?'

'Right! So the someone could be anyone. Actually,' Sarah said, 'it's all rather worrying when you think about it. Seems a pity when you and Ant have got so much to worry about already.'

Simon's reaction was astonishing. He waited until after dinner, when Jonathan was upstairs asleep and they were watching television. The Alexandrine credits of *Twin Peaks*, which like a wounded snake dragged their slow length along, had reached no more than the third vertebra when he got jerkily out of his armchair, switched off the television set, cleared his throat and said, 'I think we should go back to London.'

'We should?'

'You and I and Jonathan. Stay in the flat for a bit.'

'But there are no facilities in the flat. He's teething. It's not like here, with just fields all round. Those people below – those Lebanese – '

'Swiss.'

'They'd complain.'

'Sarah, people living in flats all over London do bring up small children. There are tower blocks of babies piled twenty-two storeys high, all teething, and the people who live there learn to put up with it. Look, you're sailing in dangerous waters; you've been told as much. And taking Jonathan with you.'

'I have to take him. I can't leave him.'

'You don't have to involve him in bloody arson. That Inspector warned you to lay off, but you wouldn't. Now you've gone too far; you've stirred things up. Maybe you didn't mean to do it, not to this extent, but you have, so you've got no option but to cool it, and the best way of cooling it, the way things are, is just to leave. We'll spend a month in the flat then go on holiday somewhere, Lanzarote or somewhere, Rhodes, Kos – anywhere it's still warm in October: I'm owed a fortnight. We can come back here when things have settled down.'

'I don't know what's got into you.'

'Someone setting fire to that car has got into me. You're alone here all day, just you and Jonathan. And some nights I've got to be away; you know that. There are people down in the village who obviously don't like what you've been doing.'

'They don't like it because they've got something to hide.'

'It's not your job to uncover it.'

'She was murdered, Simon.'

'You're not a policeman.'

'I'm better than the police. I'm more concerned than the police.'

She had astonished herself. She was shouting at him. It was exhilarating; she ought to do it more often. The whole point of living in a house in the country surrounded by fields, she realised, was that you could shout at your husband and no-one would hear.

He stared at her then looked quickly up at the ceiling. Sarah's exhilaration passed. Everything – everything! – had to be referred in some way to that baby. She would go mad without relief.

Simon said, 'It isn't a question of being better; you're not in competition with the police. It's a question of whose job it is. If whoever killed that girl – all those years ago, Sarah – if that person is still alive, and he and his friends in the village are prepared to break into someone's garden and set fire to the evidence, then you're in danger as the police are not.'

'You think I've been competing?'

'What else? Holding back information. Trying to go it alone. What are you trying to prove? Why can't you settle for what you've got?'

'And what have I got?'

'A husband. A child. A home. You're not exactly short of occupation, for Christ's sake. There's enough to do, just looking after Jonathan and running this place.'

'That defines me, does it?'

'Don't do a feminist number on me, Sarah. Give me credit. I'm not knocking what you do; it's important. I'm not suggesting I could do it, though I agree with you; I ought to try – more than I do. But you don't give yourself credit either. You think I undervalue what you do, but it's you putting yourself down. Believe me, I know about the attention, the concentration, the understanding . . . sympathy . . . the patience. . . . Human relations is my job, but I'd never be able to cope with what you have to do full-time.'

Sarah wondered briefly whether a swift kick in the balls might be the best way of dealing with this garbage. Instead she said, 'Okay. I'm not asking you to cope with what I do, not full-time, not all of it. But you want us to go back to town for a bit, right? Well, if we do, we'll have a new arrangement. Work-sharing: that's the answer. I'll give up competing with the police, and we'll both work part-time and share looking after Jonathan.'

'If I could, I would. But just tell me any way in which each of us working half a week will bring in fifty thousand a year.'

'Work from home, then. Get a computer terminal. That's how it's done these days.'

He had that patient look which he never assumed in an argument until he knew he had won it. 'I could not work from home, Sarah, because my work is meetings. It is all meetings. Promotions is human interface. It cannot be done at home. I'm in the people business.'

'You want me to be a wife and mother, right? That's enough for me?' This was unfair, she knew. She had herself accepted the role, embraced it even, and certainly it filled the time. But it was not a moment for fairness. People in the people business turned fairness to their advantage.

'It's not such a bad thing to be.'

'I'm a human being. I've got a brain, and I ought to use it.' Sarah could hear her mother speaking, but decided she didn't care.

'Nobody's stopping you. You don't have to go out to a job to use your brain. Write a novel or something; you've got imagination – far more than me. Paint watercolours. Do a course at the Open University. Jimmy Barlow's wife is studying Psychology. She says she'll begin a new career when the kids grow up. I mean . . . .' Hands spread out in a gesture of generosity; he was in the people business. 'If it's a question of an au pair, we can manage it; we've talked about it often enough. You've always been the one against it.'

'Yes, I have.' She had no desire to share her house or Jonathan with any teenage French delinquent. She had no desire to go back to London either; she had grown used to the fields and the silence. She would not give up the hunt for Dorrie's murderer. It was not competition with the police; it was an emotional commitment to Dorrie, a kind of identification. Simon himself had so little capacity for identification, people business or not, that he could not understand that. As for the Inspector, he had no feeling for Dorrie whatever.

Yet Simon had to be given something. How could she get to him? What did he want? 'You really believe that whoever set fire to the car is capable of coming up here and attacking me or something?'

'I don't know. I think it's possible. I don't want to take the chance.'

'He would be over sixty.'

'He seems to have friends.'

Right! He did believe it, he was worried, but mainly because he thought he ought to be. To do Simon justice, his nature was not directive. Sarah said, 'If I tell the Inspector everything I know, will that satisfy you? Nobody's going to come after me, if the police know as much as I do. I really don't want to go back to town, Simon. I don't want to do work-sharing or anything. I like it here, and anyway the French beans and courgettes need eating. They'll be cropping for a month at least.'

'I still think you'd be safer getting out of here for a bit.'

He had given in; the bargain had been made. Sarah said, 'I'll think about it. I'm going to bed now,' and went.

Simon stayed up to watch the snooker. When he came to bed, he said, 'Well, I'm glad that's cleared the air.' But it had not cleared the air. It had simply created a necessity to deceive, which would not be particularly difficult since Simon spent so little time in his own home.

The Inspector listened carefully to what Sarah had to tell him, and made notes with a gold pencil in a small leather-covered book. He uttered no reproach, assigned no blame, and his few questions were factual. When she had finished, he said, 'I find that very interesting, Mrs Arnott. Extremely helpful.'

'I thought you might be angry.'

'I'm rarely angry, except with my colleagues and some local politicians. If I allowed myself to become angry with members of the public, I'd be in a permanent froth. The secret is to expect very little. "God gave her a precious gift, and she took it to the marketplace." Well, we know what that means, don't we?'

'Do we? You've been asking the questions. Has anyone said as much to you? Even hinted at it?'

'Not in so many words. But the fact that she was pregnant is an indication. Promiscuity was more of a problem in those days. No pill, not much enthusiasm – then as now – for using a condom, and *coitus interruptus* has never been a very satisfactory method of contraception.'

'How far have you got with finding the father?'

'Not very far, perhaps for that very reason. Too many candidates.'

'Have the village people actually said there were too many candidates?'

'No. Generally speaking they've given me no leads at all. Which would be the case if there were too many candidates – too many people with something to hide. If there was only one candidate, I'd have more of a chance.'

'What did the children say?'

'What children?'

'The ones she taught. You told me they remembered

her. You said she rescued Billy Garbett and his sister from the snow. Have you talked to them about her? Not about whether she existed: I know you did that. About *her*. They'd know what she was like – have their own view of her anyway.'

The Inspector shifted in his seat. She had assisted him with his enquiry; he was unwilling to put her down. 'Very ingenious!' he said. 'Children nowadays – yes, I agree; they are knowing, taken by and large: I blame the television. You've suggested something to me there; it's an area we're liable to neglect. One would have to be wary, of course; they fantasise a lot. Still. . . . But this was forty-two years ago. Children in those days were much more innocent. I think you'd find she was just the teacher to them – someone above them. And even if that were not the case, Mrs Arnott, I don't know how much you can remember about your own childhood.'

She could have persisted, could have maintained her own view that children have never been innocent, have always seen more and differently, and that, if he were not so far from his own childhood, he would remember this. She could have said that there are some childhood memories that stick for ever, and that the right question, a little encouraging nudge even to someone over fifty is liable to bring a whole tumble of recollections in response. But Sarah no more wished to put the Inspector down than he her. She was too grateful to him for receiving her confession of duplicity so calmly, and also it seemed to her that they might now have reached a point at which they could begin to share. 'Anyway,' she said, 'why bother? We're almost there now, aren't we?' The new sharing caring Inspector never even raised an eyebrow at that 'we'. 'All we've got to do is find out who set fire to the car.'

'I'm not sure I follow you.'

She was surprised. He had taken the notes; he must have followed the logic. 'The epitaph was on the car. Whoever burned the car wanted to destroy the epitaph. You'd been asking questions about Doris Reeves, trying to discover who might have been the father of her child. The epitaph, in some way we haven't figured out yet, pointed to the father. He had to destroy it – or get someone else to destroy it. Instead of a murder in 1948 we've got arson in 1990, but either way when you solve one, you've solved the other.'

'Yes, I see. Ingenious! I hadn't been thinking along those lines myself, I'm bound to say.' Was this man worthy of her? She had hoped for Inspector Parker to Lord Peter Wimsey, and all she was getting was Inspector Japp to Poirot. He looked at his watch. 'Ah! Lunchtime. He might be home. Do you mind if I use your phone? There's one in the kitchen, isn't there? I shan't be a moment.'

He returned, rubbing his hands in a state of high satisfaction, very different from the washing action of Wendy and Mrs Partridge. 'He's on his way.'

'Who is?'

'Local man. Village bobby. Lucky to find him in.' He laughed. 'Better than finding him out, eh? But he's a good lad. Been quite useful.'

'Is this the butter-coloured one who came when we discovered the skeleton, or the bearded one who helps old ladies when they fall out of bed and their husbands can't get them back?'

'Does he do that? It's not in the job description. Good public relations, though. Worth the effort.'

It was the bearded one. He sat straight upright in a chair designed for lounging, and refused all refreshment, remarking pointedly that his dinner was being kept hot for him. The Inspector said, 'This business of the fire at the Old Vicarage. I'm told you've cleared that up.'

'Unofficially, sir.'

'Best way.'

A reassuring smile from the senior to the junior policeman,

the Inspector's equivalent of a fatherly hand on the shoulder, though in fact the two men were of an age. They were playing a game with her. Sarah said, 'But it was reported officially. By Mr and Mrs Bazely.'

'That's right. Didn't get far. There's two lines of operation, you see, in a village. Unofficial's the one that gets results.'

'You've charged someone, then?'

'No.'

'Make it official, that would,' said the Inspector. 'Last thing you'd want in an unofficial enquiry. Tell Mrs Arnott what happened, Tom.'

'Confidential matter, sir.'

'Special circumstances.'

So he told her. In cases of vandalism, he said, he usually had a pretty good idea who was most likely responsible; there was a limited pool of disruptive adolescents in the locality. All that made this case different was the extent of the damage, which had been well beyond what was usual. Had to be a reason for that. He'd had a word in various ears and discovered that recently Mr Bazely, driving back from Birmingham on his own, had given a lift to a local lad whose motorbike had broken down. During the course of their ride together, Mr Bazely had placed his hand on the lad's thigh, and made certain suggestions. The fire in the vicarage garden was the result, an expression of outrage you might say, the work of the lad himself and some friends he preferred not to name. Tom had since had a private word with Mr Bazely, who had decided not to press charges. The matter might therefore be considered closed.

'How do you explain the cupid?'

'Sorry?'

'They put a lead cupid on the fire.'

'They put all sorts on the fire.'

'All sorts of wood. To burn. This was lead. It melted.'

'It was moveable, Mrs Arnott. Valuable. They put it on the fire. Simple as that.'

'It blotted out . . . effaced . . . .'

She looked sideways at the Inspector. If Gary had gossiped in the village, then the presence of the epitaph on the Morris Eight was common knowledge already, but even so . . . . The Inspector came smoothly into action. 'Thank you, Tom. We won't keep you from your dinner.'

When the bearded policeman had gone, Sarah said, 'It won't do, you know. They deliberately destroyed the epitaph. There was a reason for that, had to be.'

'It will do, Mrs Arnott. It'll do very well for me. I'd like you to follow *my* logic, if you please. Just after the war, there was a young lady lodging at the vicarage and teaching at the school. She called herself Doris Reeves, and that may have been her name, but she lied about where she came from and her past generally, which is hardly an indication of good character, and that inscription you found seems to bear it out that she was *not* of good character. The vicar and his wife were childless, which suggests that there may have been something wrong with the sexual side of their marriage. You have a provocative young lady. living in close contact with a frustrated man, who was himself still young. She became pregnant. We've been looking for a father – do we need to look further?' Sarah opened her mouth to say, 'Yes, much further. I've already covered most of this ground,' but the Inspector rolled on over her. 'Given so much, what follows? Blackmail. "She took her talent to the marketplace", eh? Well, you're right; our enquiries haven't thrown up any suggestion of prostitution, though it can't be ruled out. But blackmail, if you think about it, is also a commercial transaction.' He was being generous now, throwing her a bone; if Sarah didn't like the idea that Dorrie was on the game, the Inspector would offer her Dorrie as a blackmailer instead. 'The vicar is desperate. He has no money, and he dare not face the scandal. Only one solution. Murder her, bury her, tell the world she's gone back to Nottingham.'

'And Mrs Partridge?'

'Accessory after the fact. Maybe helps to bury the girl, certainly helps with the cover-up – got no choice, poor woman, or thinks she hasn't. They're a Christian couple. I've no doubt he says a few words over the body once they've put it in the ground, but they can't erect a memorial to Doris Reeves where they've buried her, so they scratch an epitaph in Latin on her car, and place it in a bower of flowers.'

'Jeremy Potter planted the clematis long after the vicar and his wife had left.'

'A minor detail, I think you'll allow. It all happened a long time ago, Mrs Arnott. The vicar's dead, and when you went up north and began to ask questions his wife committed suicide.'

'Are you telling me you're closing the file?'

'No, not when I can't positively identify the corpse; it'll have to stay open. But I'm putting it on the back burner, as you might say. With the IRA on the loose in the Midlands and war coming in the Persian Gulf – with all the aggravation *that's* liable to cause on the home front for an overworked police force – I've got too much to do to go chasing after murderers who are already dead.'

EXTRA TUITION

Dorrie said, 'What do you know about me? You know nothing about me.' Hitherto the Dorrie of Sarah's dreams had always possessed a full set of physical features, although, if put to it, Sarah could not have described them. Now she had no face, no body, no corporal presence at all; she had been reduced to a voice inside Sarah's head. What had not been reduced was her capacity for reproach. Sarah did not even have to be in bed asleep: Dorrie could enter her mind at any time, particularly if Sarah happened to be engaged in some way with Jonathan – feeding him, changing him, bathing him, amusing him, putting him to bed. Sarah began to fear that Dorrie might be able to enter Jonathan's mind also, might even be trying to take over as a substitute for the child dead in her womb, but there was no way of telling, since Jonathan, although one might pretend that the sounds he made were the beginnings of speech, did not actually talk yet.

She telephoned the Home at Temple Glazeby, but Miss Hedges, although better, was not yet well. Sarah said she would come over on Wednesday and hope to be allowed to visit.

She took Jonathan and went again to the vicarage. Was her intention to confront Ant? She did not know; she had to do something. The bearded policeman had not said that

Ant had confessed to making a pass at the motorcyclist, only that he had decided not to press charges. She found Wendy alone in Ant's study, packing books into a tea-chest.

'You've heard?'

'Where is he?'

'Digs in Birmingham. We've put the house on the market; I'm staying here until we sell it. He won't. Can't bear to be seen in the village; he's too ashamed. I said, "What is there to be ashamed about? If it'd been a teenage girl, nobody would have been surprised; there'd have been no complaints." But he won't see it like that.'

'Did he admit . . .?'

'No, of course not. They'd have had to charge him if he had. But as things are, if it came to a trial, it would be Ant's word against the boy's. They couldn't convict him, but it'd be very messy. By agreeing not to press charges about what those kids did to the garden, we avoid all that. Keeps it out of the newspapers. Not that we'd rate anything more than the *Leamington Courier*.' Wendy had not bothered to make up this morning. The skin of her face was grey, her lips pale, her eyes now revealed as a little too small. 'But if what you're asking is did he do it, of course he did. It's happened before. Always when he's under strain. I suppose I hoped that the business with the car and the Latin might have distracted him, but it was too late, and anyway he didn't like you coming here.'

'Why not?'

'Afraid I might make a friend, I suppose. He doesn't like me making friends. Threatens the relationship.' She noticed Sarah's expression, and said, 'No, no, nothing like that. We're not a cover for each other; life might be less complicated if we were. Ant's not gay, except for the occasional pass at a biker when he's feeling particularly low in self-esteem, and I'm not lesbian. It's communication that makes Ant jealous. Just ordinary friendship. Anyone else on the island.'

'You accept that?'

'I settle for it. I might feel the same, I suppose, if Ant . . . . Not that Ant ever does make friends, except professional friends, and not many of those, and they don't last beyond the job, which is the advantage of them for Ant. Christ! Do I sound like a bitch?'

'No.'

'I must do.'

'You sound desperate, Wendy.'

'Well, I am. We both are. Desperate . . . frightened . . . not just about the job. Frightened of going on as we are, and frightened of being alone. You're lucky; you've got a kid. But Ant's the child in our case; I don't think I could cope with another. Do *you* think you're lucky?'

Sarah looked down at Jonathan, not in his mood-catching mode for once, felt the purest gooeyness rising like a warm tide inside her, and knew that, in spite of all inconvenience, she was lucky. 'Yes,' she said, 'I'm lucky.' Wendy had not suggested that Sarah was lucky in having Simon for a husband, but Wendy had not met Simon. 'What will you do?' she said.

'Find somewhere else to live. We paid too much for this place; Ant said we had to get out of the rat race. We'll probably take a loss on it. But if the programme packs up, we'd have had to move anyway.'

She had a little movement with her chin she made from time to time, almost like a tic, except that, Sarah realised, what Wendy was doing was keeping her chin up, but she had been doing it for so long that it had become habitual. She realised also that what she felt for Wendy, and had done without knowing it since their first meeting, was affection and a fellow-feeling. She said, 'I don't believe that setting fire to the Morris Eight was anything to do with Ant and the biker.'

'The village bobby does.'

'Do you?'

'The boy confessed.' Wendy placed a copy of Halliwell's *Television Companion* carefully in the tea-chest, and reached out for *Roget's Thesaurus* and *The Which Book of Money*. 'You think it's too convenient?'

'I think somebody took advantage of what Ant did, and if it hadn't been that, it would have been something else. I don't say the boy didn't do it, but I think he was put up to it. I think he had help.'

'A group of them, the bobby said. Vandalism's a group activity, usually performed after drink.'

'There was a lot of planning. Bringing the fencing and the petrol. Taking the garden gate off its hinges. Piling the wood inside the car as well as out. And then the cupid.'

Wendy's face had lost a little of its grey colour. She rummaged around among the books, and found a spectacle-case. 'Thinking glasses!' she said. The spectacles had no-nonsense square lenses in black frames. They caught the light and glittered. In her thinking glasses, Wendy became a decision-maker. 'You're right. That cupid was round the corner in the vegetable garden. They had to go looking for it. Everything else was from the back.'

'And then they placed it carefully just where it would blot the epitaph out when it melted. Okay, everyone in the village knew about the epitaph once Gary had shot his mouth off – '

'Once I had.'

'My fault. I should have told you more.'

Wendy said, 'I haven't had any breakfast, if you don't count cigarettes. Let's make a lot of toast. Does Jonathan like Marmite?'

'Too much salt. He might suck on a soldier if we cut the crust off.'

'We'll try it.' They made coffee and a whole regiment of buttery soldiers, on one of which Jonathan sucked, and sat companionably at the kitchen table. Wendy said, 'I'll miss this place. I'm not suggesting we've been happy here, but I like the place. What does your Inspector say?'

'That's the problem.'

So it all came spilling out, what had happened and what was now not going to happen and Sarah's own utter bewilderment at what to do next. Wendy's eyes moved thoughtfully behind the thinking glasses as she listened, and she chewed her top lip and butter ran down her chin. Finally she said, 'When he told you . . . back at the beginning . . that asking questions might be dangerous . . . he was right, you know. Because look what's happened to us.'

It came to Sarah that what had happened to Wendy and Ant was her fault, that the whole messy business of Ant's unskilful pass at the biker might have been passed over, if she, Sarah, had not come looking for clues in Dorrie's car, and found the epitaph. 'Oh, Christ! I'm sorry,' she said.

Wendy shook her head. 'He was working up to something. It always does end in some kind of catastrophe. And as for this place, we couldn't have afforded the interest on the mortgage much longer; we'd have had to sell. No, what I mean is, it's two-edged.'

'What's two-edged.'

'The police giving up. On the one side, you've lost their help – not that you were giving each other much help anyway; as you say, you didn't exactly share information.'

'I just hoped we might.'

'That hope has fled. Don't think you can revive it, not without something really solid in the way of evidence, and even that wouldn't do much good; the police don't like being proved wrong. But on the other side, you've got a free hand now, haven't you?'

'Not exactly free if there's still an elderly murderer out there on the loose. That's what's been worrying Simon. Wendy, I don't think I've ever eaten as much toast as this.'

'Me neither. It's very moreish. I'll make another couple of slices.'

'Not yet. Tell me about this free hand.'

'Just let everybody know the police have given up because the vicar did it, and he's dead. That's where the Latin points, after all – points straight to the Rev. Case solved. The village people know about the Latin, right? – because Gary's told everyone. And they think they know why the local vandals made a fire in our garden, right? – because Ant made a pass at one of their brightest and best. If your murderer put the vandals up to it, he didn't say, "Destroy this evidence for me"; he said, "Take your rightful revenge on this media pervert, and make sure you destroy everything valuable in his garden, particularly the disgusting lead statue in the shape of a naked boy." And now even the murderer – once he knows the police reckon they've solved the case because the vicar did it – well, he may think he wasted his time getting the epitaph destroyed, but it doesn't matter because the point is, he's safe. And if he's safe, love, then you're safe, provided you give yourself a good excuse for asking a few more questions.'

'Where did you get those thinking glasses? I want a pair.'

'It's not just the glasses. It's the little grey cells behind.'

Before she left, Sarah said to Wendy, 'You and Ant . . . . What you've drifted into . . . I don't know how it was when you started, but now . . . it's like two unpopular kids at school. They go around together because they'd rather have each other than nobody.'

'Right!'

'Trouble is . . . if you cling together too tightly . . . nobody else can get in anyway. So it will never change?'

'Right!'

'Unless you can persuade Ant to be a bit less

exclusive, wouldn't you be better giving it a go on your own?'

And Wendy said, 'Too late!'

> Sept 9th, 1946: School re-opened after the summer holidays. Six of the seniors have left and five infants enrolled, making a total enrolment of 65 children. Miss D. Reeves from Nottingham, who is awaiting entrance into a Training College, has taken up temporary teaching duties at the school, and has been placed in charge of the Infants.

It was a thick book, bound in black cloth, with a reinforced spine and marbled endpapers and the words 'LOG BOOK' stamped in gold on the front. The lined paper inside was coarse and yellow like that of a school exercise-book, though each of the three hundred pages was numbered at the top, and there was an Index at the front of the book which had not been used. The entries were handwritten and dated; they had not been made daily – sometimes there was a week between them – but only when there was some occasion to be recorded. Many of them were repetitious, the same words over and over again to describe the same occasions. The Attendance Officer visited roughly every fortnight, the School Doctor and the Dentist twice a year, the District Nurse examined the heads of the children for lice at the beginning of every term, and fruit juices were distributed to the children once a month. Which fruit juices, and why only once a month, when vitamin C is used up by the body within a day? Were the children lined up like orphans to receive a glass each or given a carton to take home? Miss Hedges did not say.

> Nov 11th, 1946: A tile has blown off the school roof. Plaster has fallen from the ceiling in the Infants' room

and rain is coming in. The Infants have been re-accommodated temporarily with the Juniors, but in spite of Miss Reeves's best efforts, cause some disruption. I have asked the vicar, Mr Partridge, the Correspondent of the Board of Managers, to inspect the state of the room. The school is in urgent need of repairs, and although the Managers have the matter under serious consideration, it seems impossible to get a contractor to come and do anything.

Dec 12th, 1946: The new Annual Intelligence Test for children born between 1st August 1935 and 31st July 1936 was held today. Five children took the Test.

Sarah began to understand the respect given by uneducated people to proper joined-up writing. This was not the scratch and scribble, the letters either disconnected or run together, the punctuation marks only loosely conjunct, of Sarah's own handwriting and that of the people she knew, even including her mother – particularly her mother. This was genuine copperplate, written in black ink with a steel nib, the up-strokes thin as a hair, the pothooks thick and curving. She remembered Miss Hedges's letter. '*Lily Partridge has made away with herself . . . .*' It was still there, if one knew and looked, though shaky now and uncertain with age and arthritis. The entries in the log book were the Hedges copperplate in its prime, each confident stroke a paradigm of calligraphy.

Feb 21st, 1947: Attendance for the week is below 50%, owing to the abnormally severe weather. It is snowing again, and conditions are getting worse. This morning two Seniors, Billy and Betty Garbett, did not arrive as expected. I telephoned Garbett's Farm and was told by their mother that they had missed the bus and set off together across the fields to the village. Miss

Reeves volunteered to look for them, and found them some way down the hill. Betty had fallen into a drift, and her brother had been unable to pull her out. She brought them to school, and they have been wrapped in towels and set by the stove to warm. Coal supplies are getting low, and there is little hope of obtaining more, owing to the bad state of the roads and the coal crisis. With the continued illness of Mr Wilkes, the teaching staff is well below strength. Miss Reeves and I divide the children between us and do what we can to instruct them. I am anxious that in particular those who will sit the Intelligence Test next autumn should not be neglected.

Mr Wilkes had reported sick on 7 February, and before that for a fortnight in January, and several times in the autumn term, though never for longer than four days at a stretch; he was clearly of a delicate disposition. But who was he and where was he now? Would the Inspector have questioned him? Sarah imagined flushed hollowed cheeks, a beard, spectacles set in rolled gold of some inferior caratage, a consumptive cough. Would Dorrie be attracted to such a man? Would she find him romantic, a kind of etiolated D.H. Lawrence? Would she choose him as the father of her child? Sarah read on, alert for clues.

March 17th: Last night's hurricane has caused great damage in the village and surrounding farms. Here at the school, the boys' tool shed has been blown over, the playground fence torn down, and we have lost several tiles from the roof. It has been impossible to get coal delivered, but with careful management and combining classes we have managed to keep the school open and, with the milder weather, attendance has improved. Mr Wilkes tells me that his father is in a critical condition after phlebitis, and that he is required to attend at the

> bedside, since Mrs Wilkes's nerves do not allow her to undertake any long periods of nursing.

Which Mrs Wilkes would this be, mother or wife? Either way, Mr Wilkes seemed to be turning into something of a wimp, and Sarah did not believe that Dorrie would fancy him. After the war, the Inspector had said, a village church school would have had to accept what teaching staff it could get.

She was reading the book – Volume Twenty-Two, 1945 to 1951, in a series that went back to 1863 – in the Staff Room, because, being an official record, it might never be taken out of the school premises, except in case of fire. As she read, she made notes, but not many; if there were indeed clues, she was missing them. Jonathan was asleep in his pram, and from time to time, almost absent-mindedly, she rocked it with one hand in order to keep him so. It had been an advantage to bring him; he had been chirrupped at by all four of the teaching staff (four now, only three in Dorrie's time, and Mr Wilkes more often away than not). The Headmaster had been particularly helpful and courteous and entirely unquestioning, and Sarah had come on strong, rather like someone putting her son down early for a minor public school, and had been shown all the facilities before retiring to the Staff Room with Volume Twenty-Two and her notebook. The staff knew that she was there and kept away, but from time to time a child would put its head round the door and Sarah would smile and wave and say, 'Sorry! Nobody in!' and the child would say, 'Thank you, miss,' and go away again.

> March 20th, 1947: The Attendance Officer and Mr Brewer, Juvenile Labour Officer, visited the school today to interview the children who are to leave at Easter. We have received the results of the '11-Plus' Intelligence Test held in December. Not one of our

> children has passed. I blame myself. The Education Authority's instructions were that, since the test is of intelligence only and not of knowledge, the children were not to be coached. But the form in which the questions were posed – though it may be quite usual among those who set such Tests –

Miss Hedges did not usually allow herself the use of dashes: her prose style was classical. Now, when anger and agitation had brought the dashes out, one could see the ink splutter.

> – was unfamiliar to our children. They were confused by the Question Paper, and did not do themselves justice. I have written to the Education Authority, but am informed that nothing can be done to rectify the unfairness. I shall enter two of the children for the Grammar School Scholarship Examination, which has not yet been discontinued, and if they should pass, I suppose that they can hardly be refused. Miss Reeves, who has been assisting with the eleven-year-olds in the absence of Mr Wilkes, is as distressed as I am, and we have consulted together on the best way to rectify the situation in future.

This was an official record, not a personal diary, yet what was already coming across was a relationship between colleagues which was personal as well as professional. It was clear that Miss Hedges had relied on Dorrie. '*We have consulted together . . . .*' Dorrie was only twenty-one in March 1947, untrained and inexperienced, and Miss Hedges was a head teacher in her forties, not much given, Sarah was prepared to guess, to consultation hitherto. But together, and with precious little assistance from the sickly, easily daunted and usually absent Mr Wilkes, they had coped with the blizzards, the blocked roads, the frozen pipes and unreplenishable coal-stocks, the hurricanes, falling attendances, holes in the roof, children lost in the snow. And a bond, an emotional bond, had been forged between them. Sarah was not imagining it; one could sense it behind the formality of the words. So why, after Dorrie had ostensibly left to have her baby in Nottingham, had Miss Hedges made no effort to keep in touch with her?

Would there be anything in the log book about the reason for Dorrie's leaving? Sarah flicked over pages quickly.

> June 29th, 1948: School closed today for the Summer Holidays, and will re-open on Tuesday, Sept 7th.

Nothing. And it was odd, wasn't it, that after the initial reference on September 9th 1946, to the 'Training College' (unspecified) to which Miss Reeves was 'awaiting entry', it was never mentioned again. She had continued to await entry for two years, which, even given the competition for places in further education after the war, seemed excessive. Sarah could understand that Miss Hedges, desperately short of staff and being offered a presentable, intelligent, likeable and competent young woman with some sort of grammar school qualification, might not have checked up on the place at a training college to begin with, but surely after the first year she would have asked, 'When exactly does your Training Course begin, Miss Reeves?'

It occurred to Sarah that one of the advantages of official language is what it can be made to conceal. 'Awaiting entry' will usually be taken to mean, 'has been offered a place at a training college, commencing at the beginning of the next academic year', but can equally well mean, 'is writing letters of application, and hopes to receive a favourable reply'. Miss Hedges need not have lied; Dorrie might have told the lie. She had lied about her home in Nottingham, and might have lied about the training centre also. And then, after a year, she had proved her worth, and Miss Hedges had not cared to ask questions because she did not want to lose her.

Nevertheless there were questions to be asked of Miss Hedges on Wednesday.

> Sept 7th, 1948. School re-opened today. Seven childen have left and there are three entrants, making a total enrolment of sixty-two children. Miss P. Harrington of London, who has recently qualified from Ashburnham College, has joined the staff to teach the Infants in place of Miss D. Reeves, who has returned to her home in Nottingham for personal reasons.

And there it was, as flat and bald as that, not even top billing.

Sarah looked back again through the book, from the point she had reached earlier. Dorrie had gone with Miss Hedges and the older children on a day's outing by coach to the seaside ('*Very few of the children have ever seen the sea, so there is a definite educational value to the excursion.*'), and, as consolation for the Infants, who had been considered too young for such excitement, had helped to organise a treat, consisting of tea, games and sports, at Hangman's Lane Farm by kind permission of Mr and Mrs Walter Barton. She had accompanied the boys' cricket team to a match with the boys of a neighbouring village school, which Radcote Boys had won, and had coached the girls for the Area Sports. When Mr Wilkes's father was buried, Dorrie had led the school choir in singing *Abide With Me* by the graveside. When one of the Infants, Jasmine Dast, had fallen in the playground and cut her chin, Dorrie had gone with Jasmine to the doctor's surgery, and held her hand while the doctor stitched her chin. When, on a chilly day late in November 1947, HRH Princess Elizabeth had married Lieutenant Philip

Mountbatten, Miss Reeves, in defiance of the Government's request that there should be no elaborate festivities in view of the financial crisis, got up a procession of the children of Radcote School to march round the village carrying loyal banners made by the children themselves, with tea and a concert afterwards in the Village Hall, at which she had operated the magic lantern.

Nowhere in the log book was it stated that Miss D. Reeves was absent because of illness or took a day off. The only school occasion of any note at which she was not recorded as having taken an active part was the Annual Exhibition and Sale of School Handcrafts in aid of Dr Barnardo's Homes, held just before Christmas. Did that mean that she went home early? If so, where was home? Could it have been, in spite of the Inspector's enquiries, Nottingham after all? Did Dorrie perhaps use another name in Nottingham?

> November 7th, 1947: The Annual Intelligence Test for Grammar School Entry was held today. Six Radcote children took the Test. Unlike the situation last year, when two of our five emerged from the Test in tears, and all were confused by the form of the questions, the children this year seem confident that they have done themselves justice. We shall see.

Since the Education Authority had forbidden coaching, one had to assume that Dorrie and Miss Hedges had not coached the children, but clearly they had been up to something.

> May 10th, 1948: Notification has been received that all six of the Radcote childen who sat for the Intelligence Test in November have passed, and will move on to the Grammar School in the autumn. I have received a formal reproof from the Educational Authority, which

> considers the result statistically abnormal. I am informed that the Test is not designed to allow all the children through, and reminded that coaching is prohibited since it would undermine the object of the Test, which is to test intelligence, not knowledge. I have replied that the Authority made no such observations when, in the previous year, all our children failed, which was just as statistically abnormal, and pointing out that, since intelligence is inherent and not acquired, no form of coaching could possibly be effective.

The note of triumph was unmistakeable and perhaps unwise in an official record. One could imagine Dorrie and Miss Hedges in helpless conspiratorial giggles together. They were two of a kind, both born teachers. '*We weren't close, but we rubbed along well enough*' – that was nonsense; the log book denied it. There had been a bond between them, a friendship, a shared joy. What had happened to break it? The pregnancy? It must have been that, but why? Yes, there were questions for Miss Hedges.

The Inspector had spoken of a school photograph. In fact there was a set of annual photographs, black-and white, taken in the summer term and pasted in an album. Sarah had the album with her in the Staff Room. Dorrie was included in two of the photographs, those for 1947 and 1948, both showing herself and Miss Hedges with the children, no sign of Mr Wilkes. She stood among the Infants, who had crowded round her, those nearest pressing against her. Her smile was a good smile, a natural smile, almost as though she were about to laugh. The teeth were a little crooked at one side, the upper lip thin but well-shaped, the lower lip generous, pointing to a dimple. The nose was small but a little too fleshy, the eyes small also, as small as Wendy's; there was no elaborate make-up in those days to compensate, certainly not for a country schoolteacher, just a hint of mascara and the faintest eyebrow pencil. Her hair was mid-length, probably chestnut, the curls probably natural, parted on the right and swept across her forehead. She wore a string of imitation pearls and a short-sleeved white linen dress with two tramlines of dark braid, probably navy, stitched to the collar and the edge of the sleeves, giving her a faintly nautical look. In the first photograph the dress was belted, in the second not, and there was a heaviness in the way she stood.

Dorrie had a face now, and a body to go with it. Sarah would have to see how far this affected the appearance of Dorrie in her dreams. Probably not very much. Most people in dreams do not have faces; we just know who they are.

There was a thin rain on the Wednesday; it was not a day for sitting under the monkey-puzzle tree. Sarah drove over to Temple Glazeby nevertheless, supposing that something would be worked out. She and Miss Hedges could not be expected to talk openly in that creepy front room, a focus of interest for all the other residents, with Ethel in the window still calling for her hearing-aid. If there was nowhere else private, they would go for a drive in the rain and talk in the car.

In the event, Miss Hedges was still not entirely well but wished to receive Mrs Arnott. Adrian took Sarah upstairs and along a corridor, past a number of what seemed to be small dormitories, each with its door open, rooms of four or six beds, each bed with its locker beside it and a curtained recess between each pair of beds for hanging up clothing. Some of the lockers had photographs in frames on top of them, some not. At the end of the corridor was a room for two, with a notice on the door, 'SICK ROOM'. Miss Hedges, propped by pillows, sat up in one bed, wearing her cardigan over a nightdress. In the other, similarly supported but by a wooden frame, was a woman (Sarah supposed her to be a woman) who looked like one of the Struldbugs in *Gulliver's Travels*. She was of immense age, almost bald under a crocheted cap through which one could see the scalp. The skin of her face was stretched tightly over her bones, but roughened in places as if by sandpaper and discoloured with liver-spots which had run into each other. Her eyes were milky with cataract, spittle leaked from the corners of her toothless mouth, and her skeletal hands moved constantly, plucking at the coverlet. Adrian sniffed, and said to Sarah, 'She needs changing. I'll do it when you've gone.'

As Adrian left and Sarah was looking uncertainly at the occupant of the other bed, Miss Hedges said, 'Don't worry. She hears very little, understands less, and remembers nothing. Practically speaking, we're alone.' And then, a little grudgingly, 'I'm glad you've come.'

'I've got a lot to tell you.'

'Well, you see I've time to listen.'

So first Sarah told Miss Hedges about the epitaph found on the Morris Eight.

Miss Hedges grunted, and said, 'I learned some Latin when I was a girl at school; we did in those days. But I can't remember it. "*Deus*" – god. "*Donum*" – gift. "*Et*" – and. "*Forum*" – does it mean the Roman Forum?'

'Marketplace.' Sarah translated the Latin, and Miss Hedges grunted again.

'Interesting!' You apply the words to Dorrie, not the car?'

'Sorry?'

'If I found a Latin inscription on an old car put out to grass – literally to grass in this case – in the garden of a country vicarage, I'd think someone was being whimsical about the car.'

Sarah had not considered this possibility, but considered it now. 'It doesn't make any sense applied to the car.'

'"God gave her a gift." I don't know how she came by the car; it certainly wasn't precious, but it could have been some kind of gift. And she did take it to the marketplace; she sold it to the Partridges.'

'If that's all, why turn it into Latin, and write it in a secret place? It still doesn't make any sense.'

'Does it make any sense applied to Dorrie?'

'I'm hoping you'll tell me.'

'What do you think it means?'

'Prostitution? That's been suggested.'

Miss Hedges shook her head. 'No question of that. She lived in the vicarage; she taught at the school. She had very little spare time and no privacy.'

'School holidays?'

The head shaken again, slowly but with even more certainty. And nothing added.

'You know that?'

'I knew Dorrie. She wasn't that kind of girl. Quite the opposite. Serious. Almost puritanical, I'd have said.'

Sarah remembered how the Inspector had teased out the information he gave, slipping in questions as he did so. The whole secret of interviewing must lie in calculating how much to tell and in what order, so as to provoke the most useful answers. Which line should she now follow, the 'Confess that you knew Dorrie much more closely than you at first led me to believe' line or the 'Doris Reeves of Nottingham never existed' line?

'Penny for them.'

It came to Sarah that, whatever line she took, it must not involve lying to Miss Hedges. She might hold back information, but not distort it. Miss Hedges had been seeing through the lies of children for most of her professional life. 'I was thinking about the school holidays. You told me she didn't get on with her mother in Nottingham, so I suppose she didn't go home. Did she stay in the village?'

'No.'

That was right; Dorrie had not attended the Exhibition and Sale of Handwork in aid of Barnado's Homes at Christmas either year, but had slipped away early. 'Do you know where she went?'

'Yes.'

This might be the jackpot, the answer to the pregnancy, the epitaph, everything. Dorrie had a secret life somewhere, and Miss Hedges knew where. Blood rushed to Sarah's cheeks and she felt dizzy. Her notebook was in her shoulder bag and she fumbled for it. She said, 'I think I might have to sit down.'

'There's no chair for visitors. Sit on the bed.'

She sat on the bed, took out her notebook carefully with hands which shook a little, and opened it, watched by Miss Hedges. The pen had fallen out of the spiral wire binding and she scrabbled for it in the bottom of the bag.

Miss Hedges said, 'You read too much into my reluctance, Sarah Arnott. You expect more than you'll get.'

Sarah said, 'There's something I should tell you. The police made enquiries in Nottingham. There was no such young woman as Doris Reeves, no such mother, no such father who had run back to Malaya. There were people called Reeves, but none of them fitted. She didn't have a home to go to in Nottingham. It was all fiction.'

'I see.' A considerable pause. 'An ingenious fiction, I think you'll agree. She used to tell stories to the children. They'd sit in a circle, and she'd ask them to suggest a subject. I was no good at all in comparison.'

'I've read the school log book. It said she was awaiting teacher training.'

'Everyone who applied in those days was awaiting teacher training. There were very few trained teachers because of the war.'

'Where did she go during the holidays?'

'To a hospital for the mentally handicapped. She worked there as a cleaner.'

'As a volunteer?'

'Paid. Your epitaph was right in one respect. Dorrie was very keen on money.' The corner of Miss Hedges's mouth twitched in a spasm of self-reproach. 'I don't mean that in any derogatory sense. Supply teachers, then as now, were badly paid, and not paid at all in the holidays. Dorrie had a passion for independence. For somebody in her position, independence could only be equated with a Savings Account. She was young, strong, and had no taste for idleness. She took what extra work she could, and saved what she made.'

'Extra work could mean . . . .'

'Read that into it if you want. I don't, and I knew her.'

'Why were you reluctant to tell me about the holiday job?'

'She didn't want anyone to know about it. I suppose that would also explain the Nottingham story; the home in Nottingham was a cover for the fact that she had no home – or none that she wanted to live in – and simply went wherever she could get work. I found out because a letter arrived for her at the school from the hospital. The name was on the back of the envelope. She asked me to keep her secret, and up to now I have done so.'

The old woman in the next bed began to laugh, and clap her hands together. Miss Hedges said, 'Take no notice. She'll stop soon.'

'Does she want anything?'

'Attention.'

'You said the letter had the name of the hospital on the back?'

'Very well, write it down in your book. St Bardolph's, Leominster. It will be another journey for you to make with your baby. I don't imagine you can push anyone to suicide there.'

It was like a blow in the face. Sarah said, 'If you don't

want me to find out who killed her – if you yourself don't want to know – why are you helping me?'

'Because you asked for help – I was a teacher, remember? And because I'm bored. And because I still need to be of use; I don't know anything else to be. Now ask another question.'

'Do you know who the father of her child was?'

'Told you before. Nobody knew – except the man himself, I suppose. The subject was much discussed, but not in her presence. She was – what? – nearly eight months gone at the end of that summer term. That means she became pregnant in November 1947. She was in Radcote then.'

'Didn't she go away for half term?'

'Good question. But half term would have been too early; we took a week in the middle of October. And anyway Dorrie stayed in the village that year, though she'd gone away the year before. But she was doing her tutoring by that time.'

'What tutoring?'

'Oh, that came out of the 11-plus. We had a good laugh about it, Dorrie and I. I told her to grab the chance and the money, as long as the school wasn't involved officially.'

Sarah had imagined the two of them laughing, and here was confirmation. 'I read about the 11-plus in the log book. You were upset.'

'It was scandalous. The children were confused. I said it must never happen again. In those days, the Test Paper was in two parts. One was Mental Arithmetic – the children knew what that was, but they were used to taking whatever time they needed; I never hurried a child. The Test Paper was against the clock. The other half was about words – "End this sequence." "Circle the words which don't belong." "Match the following words into pairs of opposites." Simple enough, but the children weren't used to it – and again it was against the clock. Dorrie said,

"Let's get them used to it." She made a game of it. They'd pick up sides, and if the question wasn't answered in so many seconds, it passed to the other side, speeding up all the time. By the next Test, all our Juniors were experts. Sailed through.'

'She charged them money for that?'

'Of course not. But the parents got to hear of it. In any school like ours at that time, those who failed the Test didn't go on to a technical school; they just stayed with us until they were fourteen. I did my best to teach them something, but there wasn't much incentive to learn, and some of them may have fallen behind. When I think of it now, I get angry – boys of thirteen taken away from school six weeks at a time in the autumn to go potato lifting! – but we took it for granted then. Some of the parents . . . the better-off . . . farmers . . . they got the idea that Dorrie was a miracle worker and hired her to give extra lessons to their offspring. She asked me what to charge, and took it on, once a week in the evenings during termtime.'

'Which parents?'

'The Bartons of Hangman's Lane were the only ones who lasted. They had trouble with their Eva; she always was a trouble, that one. Whether she was backward because she didn't want to learn or didn't want to learn because she was backward, I couldn't tell; they'd call it dyslexia these days. Dorrie struggled with her for several months and thought she'd made some headway, but it was a battle of wills.'

Sarah wrote it down. 'Eva . . . Barton . . . I'd like to talk to her.'

'No reason why not. She still lives in the village. She married Tom Potter; he worked for her father.'

'You don't mean old Mrs Potter – Jeremy's grandmother?'

'Oh, you know Jeremy, do you? I remember him well – a bright little boy, much brighter than his father, but a little too anxious to please.'

'He's bigger now.'

'I don't know why you call Eva old. She's not old. She can't be sixty. Left school when she was fourteen, December 1947. I couldn't do much with her, but her father was obstinate – hence the tuition. Only child, you see, and he'd quarrelled with his brother.'

'But the village calls her old Mrs Potter.'

'They've got to, haven't they? There are three of them; they must be distinguished. There's Eva; that's Tom Potter's wife; that's old Mrs Potter, has to be, though she's not old. And there's Mrs Potter; that's Beattie, Mrs Walter Potter, Jeremy's mother. And then there's young Mrs Potter; that's Mrs Jeremy Potter. You can call people old, but it doesn't mean to say they are old.'

'But she looks old.'

'Well, of course she does. All the women in that family age very quickly. They age, but they don't die. The men die. Good God, Sarah Arnott, you're talking about a woman who has a great-aunt still alive, and in this very room with you. Hannah Barton. Say hullo to Hannah.'

Sarah turned and stared at the old woman in the next bed who cawed, nodding her head vigorously and flapping her hands. Miss Hedges said, 'Hannah, we're talking about you.' The old woman set up a wailing. 'Now we're not.'

There was a knock at the door and Adrian entered without waiting to be invited in; it was possible that he had been listening at the keyhole. He clicked his tongue. 'You've upset her.'

Miss Hedges said, 'Nonsense! Quite the contrary! I gave her a good verbal swipe when she walked on some tender ground, but she's over it now, aren't you, my dear?'

'Not talking about you two. Sorry, Mrs Arnott. Look at Hannah, listen to her. That'll go on for hours if it's not stopped.'

'Change her, then. We'll turn our backs.'

Sarah said, 'I really must go. You've given me a lot to think about. I'll come back next week, if I may.' That tender ground had been Lily Partridge's suicide, for which Miss Hedges clearly did hold Sarah at least partially responsible, but the fact that she had been able to mention it to Adrian in indirect apology might indicate that it did not rankle. 'Is there anything you'd like me to bring?'

'A name. Tell me whodunnit.'

'That may take longer than a week.'

'You've roused my interest, Sarah Arnott.'

Sarah said, 'You'll know when I know, I promise.'

The rain had stopped. As she reached her car, she saw that there was a man in a balaclava helmet, wearing a yellow waterproof cape over jeans and a sweater, clipping the hedge. He waved at her, and grinned. 'Afternoon, Mrs Arnott!' It was Clyde. Did Jeremy have a contract to maintain the grounds of the old people's Home, or was Clyde moonlighting? Sarah remembered that he lived at Temple Glazeby.

She said, 'I hardly recognised you. You look like a bank-robber.'

Clyde said, 'Oh, I'm a tearaway when I'm on home ground.'

What had Clyde been doing, in his balaclava, on the night of the fire in the vicarage garden?

Shut up, Sarah Arnott, and get on home. You've got plenty to think about.

The arithmetic did not add up.

Elsie had gone home. Sarah lay on the living-room carpet beside her son and tickled his tummy.

'Doesn't add up, chicko,' she said. 'There's holes in this.' Jonathan was on his cot blanket over a waterproof sheet to protect the carpet. He did not need changing. The smell which came off him was of milk and baby-breath and machine-washed rompers which had all sorts of additives to make them spring-fresh and bouncy. It was an aroma positively guaranteed to entice a mother into placing her face an inch above her baby's tummy, blowing into his navel, shaking her head and making bubbabubbabub noises while being struck repeatedly on the back of the neck by a plastic rattle.

Jeremy, as Sarah knew, was twenty-three, the oldest of three siblings. 'Therefore,' she said, moving on to her side and using Jonathan's fingers to illustrate her calculations, 'He was born in 1967.' Jonathan nodded his agreement, and Sarah continued to work backwards through the years. Jeremy's father, Walter (named presumably for Eva's father, Mr Walter Barton of Hangman's Lane, from whom the farm had been inherited), had been married at eighteen. 'Allow some time – okay? – maybe not as much as nine months, but part of a year – ' Jonathan was prepared to allow part of a year, if not the full nine months, between Jeremy's father's marriage and Jeremy's own birth. ' – and then go back eighteen years to Jeremy's father's birth, that's Walter Potter, son of Tom and Eva, and we're in late 1948 or early 1949, only a few months after Dorrie's death.'

This was much too complicated a process of reckoning for Jonathan, who threw his rattle as far as he could (which was luckily not very far) in a vaguely westerly direction. Sarah retrieved it. Jonathan's attention span was too short to qualify him as a detective's sidekick. Doctor Watson, Captain Hastings, they may not have been very bright, but they did at least listen and try to follow what was said. It seemed to Sarah that, as a housewife and mother, she was disadvantaged in almost every way when it came to detection. 'I don't complain, though, you notice,' she said, returning the rattle to Jonathan who immediately threw it away again. 'Point is, Eva Barton was only fourteen at the end of 1947, and Dorrie was giving her extra tuition in early 1948. Now Jeremy told me his grandfather was twenty-four when he married his boss's daughter. Didn't bother to mention that his gran was only fifteen.'

'*Married the boss's daughter. Takes longer.*' In fact it hadn't taken any time at all. Nowadays Eva would still have been at school. It would have been a marriage of necessity, of course; he would have made her pregnant; it began to seem to Sarah that there had been a lot of unexpected pregnancies in the village back in 1948. It must have caused a great deal of aggro in the Barton family – an only child, and her father had wanted the best for her, had engaged a private tutor to improve her education, and then she had been put in the club by his own farm labourer, who had, on Walter Barton's death, inherited the farm.

The village women who were in their late fifties, though they had grown-up children and grandchildren too, did not consider themselves old. They watched television and subscribed to women's magazines and read the articles on fashion in the weekly colour supplements of various newspapers, shopped in Stratford, Leamington or Warwick, and knew what was what. They were mature experienced women, able and willing to attract a man. They dyed their gray hair blonde or black or various shades of red or brown, and some even chose lavender, and one had chosen pink. In this they resembled women of their age all over the country; the village style might be provincial but was not frumpish.

But old Mrs Potter (born Eva Barton) did not dye her hair, wore very little make-up, and she dressed and behaved much older than her years. 'All the women in that family age,' Sarah said to her son. 'They age, but they don't die. That's not it, though, with Eva, is it, my lad, not it at all?' This ageing was by choice, not by nature. It was as if Mrs Tom Potter had decided that the nine-year difference between herself and her husband simply did not exist.

Jonathan lay on his back on his cot blanket, his head

propped up by a cushion. He had been waving his arms and legs roughly in time with her voice as she explained the intricacies of the Barton/Potter time-scheme to him, but now suddenly he stopped all movement and became utterly still, his gaze fixed as if on something which was happening out of the window. Sarah's gaze followed his, but nothing was happening outside the window except weather. The moment passed. Jonathan decided that it was time to make his own contribution to the conversation, which emerged as a string of gibberish well-lubricated with spittle. His arms and legs began to move again, faster than before. Sarah's eyes filled with tears. It was old Hannah Barton there on the blanket, mopping and mowing, talking gibberish and flapping her hands. She reached out to Jonathan and held him close while he protested and his mother wept. She had looked into the future and seen what time would do to her son, and knew that she could not prevent it.

There was also the question of how to tell Simon that she had to go to Leominster.

ON THE BACK BURNER

It was probably a mistake to tackle old Mrs Potter at the butcher's shop, particularly since, as Sarah later realised, Rob was a Barton himself, and therefore some sort of kin to her. Also there were two other customers in the shop. One was a a very old woman, unknown to Sarah, who was buying Rob's own pork 'n beef sausages in a quantity sufficient to feed several generations of an extended family, but buying them one at a time, giving prolonged consideration to every request to add another sausage to the pile already on the scales. The other was one of the council-house wives, a recent arrival, urban overspill not yet accepted in the village.

Rob was slicing ham very thin for the urban overspill, while Geoff, his young assistant, with the patient cheerfulness which was his most singular characteristic, served the old woman. Geoff was a black belt at judo, who had achieved inner contentment through self-abnegation and the pursuit of excellence, and now gave classes in it at the Youth Club. Old Mrs Potter was next in line, so Sarah, coming in and finding her there becalmed, seized the moment.

'Hullo, Mrs Potter. I'm so glad to see you. I've been hoping to talk to you.'

An instant stiffening and a half-turn of her head. 'What

about?' The ears of everyone else in the shop pricked up. Sarah already began to realise that yet again she had made a mistake. Would she ever learn how to approach the village people?

'I expect you know that the police have identified that skeleton which was found in our garden.'

'Why should I?'

A part of Sarah wanted to reply, 'Because everyone in the village knows that the police have been asking questions about Doris Reeves, and if you say you don't, you're a liar,' but a soft answer turneth away wrath, so she only said, 'Well, they're pretty sure she was somebody called Doris Reeves who used to teach at the village school. And now they know who killed her,' – raising her voice to make absolutely sure that everyone in the shop heard this bit – 'and it seems he died eight years ago, so they've closed the case. But I thought I'd like to find out a bit more about her – what kind of person she was, that sort of thing.'

'Why?'

'Proprietary interest.'

'What's that when it's at home?'

This was going wrong; the hostility was almost palpable. 'Interest. Just interest. She was on our land. I thought perhaps I might come round and see you.'

'You've no call to do that. I never knew the woman.'

'But she taught you, surely?'

'Taught a lot of people. Taught at the school. You said so.'

The very old woman had stopped buying sausages, at least for the moment, and had turned up her hearing-aid. The urban overspill paid for her ham and left the shop, but Rob did not wish to interrupt such an interesting conversation, so he busied himself in pretending to bone a shoulder of lamb instead of coming forward to ask Mrs Potter what she wanted.

'But she taught you particularly, didn't she? Private tuition. She came to your father's farm once a week.'

'Who told you that?'

'Miss Hedges.'

'Taught me nothing. She may have come round. Nothing to do with me. A woman like that, what could she teach me? Worth nothing. Came out of nowhere and went back where she came from. You'd do better to mind your own business and leave her where she lies.' Where did Dorrie lie now? Had the Forensic people returned her bones to the police? Buried them? Burned them? How could she be interred, written off, registered as dead, when there was no absolute certainty who she was? Old Mrs Potter spoke to Rob. 'You serve Mrs Arnott. I'll come back when you're not so busy.'

Rob left the shoulder of lamb and came forward. Sarah said, 'I'm sorry. That's twice I seem to have offended her, and both times in your shop. I don't know why.'

Rob said, 'Been talking to Miss Hedges, have you? She taught me at school. Always something to say for herself, that one. Good teacher, though. She was well respected.'

Sarah said to Jeremy, 'I'm afraid I got off on the wrong foot with your grandmother.'

'I heard.'

Sarah said to Simon, 'I might be going to Leominster.'

'Might be?'

'Shall be.'

'When?'

'Don't know yet.'

'Why?'

'Something Miss Hedges told me.'

'You're not planning to take Jonathan?'

'Can't very well leave him.' She had, in fact, seriously considered leaving Jonathan with her mother. It would be bad, of course – he might consider it a rejection, which would lead to trouble in later life – but viewed in relative terms was not as bad as leaving him with Simon's mother.

Simon said, 'You're still obsessed by that bloody skeleton, aren't you? Well, I won't have it.'

This was the first time in their married life when Simon had ever forbidden her to do anything, so it was clearly a serious moment and must be handled with care. Sarah said, 'I don't see that you've got any choice.'

'Of course I've got a choice.'

'You going to stop me going? Tie me down? Close the joint account so that I haven't any money?'

'I'm asking you not to go.' And that, objectively considered, was all he could do. His error lay in thinking that asking was all he had to do. It was a hangover from earlier times; a bit of Simon still believed that his word was her command. 'Look,' Simon said, 'I'm not one of those husbands; you know I'm not. I've never tried to impose on you. You've always gone your own way.'

This was a lie. For most of their life together she had gone his way, but by her own choice. 'But?'

'But I'm not allowing you to carry Jonathan all over the country on some wild-goose chase.'

'If it's only a wild-goose chase he's in no danger, so why shouldn't he come with me?'

'You promised you'd give this whole thing up.'

'I promised I'd tell the Inspector everything I knew, and I did. As a result, he's put the whole case on the back-burner. I haven't. Look, if it's just Jonathan you're worried about, I'll leave him with you. You can stay at home and look after him. Proper fathering – it'll do you good.'

Simon pushed away his plate. 'I don't want any more of

this. I'm going to bed. I've got to be up early in the morning.'

So ended the first stage of their battle.

Since breakfast for Simon was a matter of a bowl of muesli and a mug of teabag tea, consumed hurriedly before driving to the station to catch the 7.25, Sarah did not join him for it; she would usually have been up at six, as well as during the night, to see to Jonathan. So hostilities were not resumed, except by silences on both sides, until after dinner the next evening; it had been agreed that they would try never to quarrel in front of Jonathan in case he picked up the vibes.

'I don't understand why you're doing this. It can't lead to anything.'

'Right.'

'Except trouble.'

'It won't lead to trouble. I've made sure the village knows that the police are satisfied they've found the murderer and he's dead, so they've closed the case. Wendy's suggestion. Takes me off the hook.'

'Confidential information, wasn't it?' This was unworthy of a reply. 'Why should the villagers believe you?'

'Because they can see it's true. No more CID, getting in everyone's hair, asking questions. All gone.'

'You haven't gone. You're still asking questions, and taking our son with you.' Simon had been well trained, not by Sarah herself, far less his mother, but presumably within the Marketing Department, where they had a check-list on sexism. He never said 'he' when making any general statement which might apply to both sexes, but always 'he or she', and he had remembered to say 'our son' not 'my son'. Brownie point to Simon. 'And now you want to take him to bloody – where is it? – Leominster. He's not a parcel.'

'Yes, he is. At this age he's a parcel. That's why we have a pram . . . pushchair . . . sling. Until he can move about by himself, he's luggage. And he goes with me; he's *my* luggage.'

'Our luggage. Very vulnerable luggage. I've told you, I won't have it.'

They didn't seem to be getting any further forward. Sarah said, 'I told you yesterday, if you don't want me to take him, stay home from the office, and look after him yourself.'

'You know I can't.'

'Take him with you to the office, then. When I worked at Bradbury and Tonge, one of the Art Directors used to bring a long-haired dachshund with him to work. She lived in a basket under his desk and barked at the juniors.'

'What happens if he gets ill on one of these jaunts?'

'There are always doctors. Hospitals. We'll be going to a hospital in Leominster, as a matter of fact. It's for the mentally handicapped, but I imagine they'll have some medical staff.'

Simon broke a glass by throwing it into the fireplace. It was a nineteenth-century U-bowl rummer, which should really have been kept for guests. He had never done such a thing before during the whole of their life together. Simon abhorred violence; Sarah was the one who broke things, though not usually things of any value. She said, 'Look, I've had an idea; it's just come to me. I'll ask Wendy to go with us. It'd be company and someone else to lend a hand with Jonathan, and she might enjoy it. How about that?'

Simon said, 'I don't understand why you're doing this. Something's got into you, maybe always been there, something deep down, something psychological. It's an obsession.'

Sarah said, 'I'm trying to find out the truth. That's not hard to understand; the truth's important.'

Simon said, 'You're my wife, Sarah. You're Jonathan's

mother. We live here – maybe not in the village itself, but certainly close. Personal relations are more important than truth. That's the first thing you learn in business.'

The third and final stage of the battle came on the third night when, after an evening spent mostly in silence, they were lying side by side in bed in the dark.

Sarah said, 'I was at the vicarage today – the bungalow where the vicar lives, not Wendy's house. I wanted to look up some dates in the parish register.'

She wasn't sure why she said this, except that one couldn't go on maintaining a silence for ever and clearly neither of them was going to sleep. To talk about Dorrie might be construed as provocative, but she did not intend to start their quarrel up again; it was just that she wanted to share a discovery and there was nobody else with whom to share it, and anyway she was not sure what it meant.

The effect on Simon was unexpected. He shouted, 'Oh, shit!' very loudly, and then turned towards her, grabbed her, and began to kiss her . . . lips, eyes, hair, ears, cheeks, throat, breasts . . . clumsily, like an inexperienced teenager who has decided to take the plunge from fevered imagination into reality, and as he hugged her to him it was clear that he was sexually aroused. Sarah was about to say, 'It's not Saturday,' but something stopped her. Instead she kissed him in return, and this calmed him – happily without causing detumescence – and he became the Simon she knew and did still love, and not the angry schoolboy who had begun the encounter.

Afterwards, with the bedside light on and Simon lying beside her but resting on one elbow so that he could look down on her, he said, 'I've been talking to a psychotherapist about you.' Sarah moved a little away, but he restrained her gently with one finger on the tip of her nose. 'I've been worried. You know I have.'

What Sarah noticed was that 'I am' had become 'I've been', but all she said was, 'Must have cost you. Psychotherapists don't come cheap.'

'Not really. Bit of a cheat. She works for us in Market Research. Delphine. She's Belgian. Apparently it's the smart thing to be.'

'What did she say?'

'She said she wasn't in the business of giving spot diagnoses about people she'd never met.' Sarah grunted, but in agreement, not disapproval, and put up one hand to touch Simon's cheek to show that she was not angry. 'She said that whether you were putting yourself in danger or not wasn't anything I could control, so I'd better let you be the judge of it. There was rather a lot about control. Delphine doesn't approve of it. She says I might as well let you go your own way, because you'd probably do it anyway, and if you didn't, that's when the real trouble would start. I'm not sure I understand all that. Then she gave me a little card with "CONCERN IS THE OTHER FACE OF CONTROL" printed on it, and threw me out.'

Sarah let her hand drop on to Simon's thigh, and thence on to his now flaccid penis, to which she gave a friendly squeeze, and Simon said, 'So tell me about the parish register.'

She had been down to the church first, and found the vicar there. This was not usual since he had to spread himself thin over four parishes and was seldom in any of his four churches except when conducting a service. However, on this occasion he had been doling out bright blue hassocks, six to a pew, from a trolley, assisted by Mrs Bertie Dast of Peacock Cottage. Mrs Bertie Dast was the renegade of that family, the Dasts being Chapel, but she compensated for her renegade state by an intense devotion to parish duties. As for the hassocks, they had been made within the village by members of the congregation and were each individually embroidered with brightly coloured flowers, birds, horses, lambs, a haywain loitering by a haystack, even a Corinthian column on a pedestal. None of the ornamentation was religious, except perhaps the lambs.

'Mrs Arnott! Welcome to God's House!' He had known who she was. Country vicars always do know who one is, even if one never goes to church. He gestured towards the trolley. 'A labour of love. We've a Christening this afternoon.'

'Do you have to do this every time there's a service?'

'Oh, yes, and gather them up again afterwards. They'd be nicked otherwise. They're all original pieces, you see, bound to attract pilferers. You'd find them turning up at Craft Fairs all over the country.'

'I'll help you.' Sarah moved Jonathan's pushchair further down the aisle, took six hassocks from the trolley, and set them in the next pew. This was not well received by Mrs Bertie Dast, who became noticeably tight-lipped. Sometimes it seemed to Sarah that she could do nothing right in the village. She had hoped to talk to the vicar on his own, but would not be able to do so without first telling him what she wanted, whereupon Mrs Dast would know, whereafter the village would know. Well, let it. 'I'm glad I've found you,' she said. 'I've been hoping to look at the parish register.'

'It's in the safe at home. I don't keep it here.' A pause. Mrs Dast's eyes went sideways. 'Any particular reason?'

'Historical curiosity.'

'You'd better come back with me, and share a crust.' It was clear from the rigidity of Mrs Dast's expression that she had never been asked to share a crust. 'There's a lot of confusion, you know, about parish registers. People have this picture of university scholars consulting mouldering manuscripts in the vestry. It's not like that at all. First, there are three registers, not one – Births, Marriages and

Funerals. Second, they aren't kept in the parish; they have to be sent to the County Record Office when they're full. So it depends how far back you want to go.'

'Late forties.'

'Ah!' Fingers drummed on the top of the trolley. 'I thought all that business was over and done with.' So he had heard. Sarah's newsflash at the butcher's had been satisfactorily disseminated. 'The police had a good look, you know. Photocopied a lot of pages. But they said, when they returned the books . . . .'

'It is. It is over, as far as I know. I'm just curious about the period.' She decided to give Mrs Dast a present, a piece of information which again she would probably already have. 'I've been reading the school log book. Fascinating!'

'Well, there's no reason why you shouldn't see the register as well. It's a public record. I can offer you soup and sardines. 'I've nothing appropriate for your little one, I'm afraid.'

'Please don't worry. There are emergency rations in the car. It's really very kind of you.'

So they had gone back together to the bungalow which now functioned as the vicarge, where they shared a tin of tomato soup, a tin of sardines and the heel of a wholemeal loaf. The vicar asked a blessing before they ate, but the bread and fishes remained obstinately insufficient.

He took a slip of paper from under the clock on the mantel, looked at it, put it back and opened the safe, which contained three leather-bound books and a silver chalice. Sarah checked three dates. Eva May Barton had been born in October 1933, had married Thomas Henry Potter in September 1948, and their child, Walter Graham Potter, had been born four months later in January 1949. That seemed to be it. Not much. Something to brood about, but not much. She would have become pregnant some time in May 1948, either while she was still receiving private tuition at her father's expense from Doris Reeves or just after Dorrie's engagement as her tutor had been terminated. The two pregnancies overlapped by three months. 'I'm afraid you won't find your skeleton in there,' the vicar said.

'No. I'm not sure what I did expect to find. It all seems a bit stark.'

'Well, I told you it would be. If you want local colour, you'll have to go to the service registers. There are hundreds of those, far too many to plough through. Far too many to keep, as a matter of fact, and I'm not bound to do so, not after a while.'

'I'm sorry. I don't understand.'

'Every service has to be recorded, not just the Christenings, Weddings and Funerals – three services a day on a Sunday, it would have been then, and often one mid-week, so it's a lot to write up. That's where you get the personal comments – attendance records and how much in the collection, anything that goes wrong, the weather, indiscipline in the choir or a stroppy organist, the heating packs up; you name it. That's your social history. We're advised always to read through the back volumes when we take a parish over. You can find out a great deal about the previous incumbent, about the congregation, and about their attitudes to each other: he can't be indiscreet, of course, but you learn to read between the lines. The period you're interested in . . . the man then . . . whatsisname . . . .'

'Partridge.'

'Now he was High. Very High. I'd guess the village didn't like it. He wouldn't have been popular.'

'How do you know?'

'Couldn't have been. This is traditionally a Chapel village. Most villages in the Midlands are. Consequently even us Anglicans tend to be Low. I'm positively Broad myself. Evangelical. The congregation are happy enough with that, as far as I can tell, though the bishop's not keen.'

'How do you know he was High?'

'Easy. What I'd call the Lord's Supper, and you might call Holy Communion, he called Mass. And there are references to incense, bits of ritual –most of which his congregation objected to – and when he wants to be cryptic he drops into Latin. He refers to himself as a priest, and it's obvious he'd have been much happier as a full-blown Roman. He could have had candles then . . . holy water . . . censers . . . handbells . . . altar-boys . . . chanting . . . everything I hate, all the show business that cuts the congregation out of the worship and comes between God and his people. Sorry! I get heated, just thinking about it.'

'But he was married.'

'Maybe that's why he couldn't go over.'

'Are you married?'

'Have been. My wife left me. Can't be sorry for that; it's how I came to find Our Lord. And my kids are grown up. Hence the tinned soup and sardines.'

'Could I see some of his service registers?'

'Be a devil to find.' Sarah realised that there were registers all around the room, being used as furniture. The vicar lifted the telephone off a pile of them, which promptly collapsed. 'Fifties! It was the late forties you wanted, wasn't it?' They found the late 1940s eventually under the sink.

And there he was, the late James Elroy, very much as the vicar had stated, as High as a kite, with falling attendances and bits of Latin (some seemed to be prayers) written in the margin, and a special devotion to Our Lady. 'Borrow a few if you like,' the vicar said. 'There's no security about these, though I'd better have them back.'

Sarah picked out the 1948 volume. While checking on the wedding between Eva Barton and Thomas Potter, about which Mr Partridge had little to say beyond a question mark in the margin, which may or may not have indicated disapproval that the bride should have been married in white, she had noticed a funeral in the same month, September. It was of someone who had lived in the Manor, Mrs Winterson, widow of Captain George Winterson, who had died two years previously. Nobody lived in the Manor now, because it had been bought for investment by a Saudi and before that a pop group had inhabited it briefly, but Sarah knew that the Wintersons had been squires of Radcote since the eighteenth century. Mr Partridge had drawn a cross in the margin very like the cross which had been scratched onto Dorrie's Morris Eight, and had used the same odd form of words, '*Requiesce in pace*' and below that, in a bracket, '*Felo de se*' which even Sarah knew, from her reading in the Crime Club collection, to mean 'a felon against oneself', in fact a self-murderer. So here was another suicide among the people of Radcote, and maybe it was just a coincidence and maybe it was not.

As she left, the vicar said, 'I know you don't come to church, so I won't harry you. But a word of warning. It can be dangerous to dig too deeply into the things of this world. I'm not sure Our Lord intended it. Safer, on the whole, to leave matters to Him.'

This was Miss Hedges again, of course – '*Vengeance is mine, saith the Lord*' – the unregenerate atheist quoting scripture to her own ends. 'What do you think about punishing war criminals fifty years on?' said Sarah.

And the vicar replied, 'Not a lot.'

It was an enormous Victorian Gothic building of gray stone with a sloping central tower, roofed with slates into which what looked like bay windows had been set. On top of the tower was a flagpole from which no banners flew. A broad flight of steps led up to the entrance, which was in the central section. On either side there were two large wings with an extension behind at each end, so that the whole building was E-shaped, with the upright of the E separated from the main road by wide lawns and flower-beds. This was the main building. Metal tablets set into the front of the tower recorded visits to it in 1871 by the Emperor and Empress of Brazil and in 1896 by the Duke and Duchess of York.

What had once been the vegetable gardens which allowed the nineteenth-century establishment to feed itself was now filled by various extensions. There was an inner semi-circle of yellow brick, built in the 1930s, and an outer semi-circle of 1960s concrete, wood and glass. One of the yellow brick buildings, Sarah noticed, had a tall chimney at one end from which dark smoke curled upwards. She thought of Belsen and shivered. Not a good beginning.

Wendy had been delighted to come with her. She hadn't had an outing for years, she said, and it would take her mind off all the grief and woe in which her life and Ant's seemed to be floundering. Grief and woe notwithstanding, Wendy was a jolly and a practical companion, and it was she who had suggested that they should read up on St Bardolph's in the *Country Guide* before going, because if one were asking a favour, one should always demonstrate that one had taken the trouble to do some homework first. Wendy had been a researcher for television before becoming a presenter, and knew what was what.

Saint Bardolph's Asylum for Idiots and Imbeciles had been built in 1868 by public subscription. The subscribers had votes allotted in proportion to the amounts they had subscribed, allowing them to elect idiots and imbeciles of their choice as inmates of the institution at no expense for periods of seven years; other inmates were privately funded and given better food and accommodation. In 1884 the title changed, and Saint Bardolph's became an Asylum for the Care, Education and Training of Idiotic, Imbecile and Weak-Minded Children and Young Persons, and in 1900 it changed again so that all the pejorative references to idiots and imbeciles were dropped, and the Asylum was now a Training Institution for the Feeble-Minded. Twenty years more and it had ceased to be an Asylum at all, or an Institution either, but became a Mental Hospital, and the inmates were patients, and continued so until the late 1980s when they began to be called 'clients' as a linguistic preliminary to closing the hospital down altogether and releasing them onto the streets of Leominster.

Sarah climbed the steps to the entrance, and found herself in a vaulted hall of the same dark stone with a double staircase immediately in front of her, at the top of which an even darker portrait in oils of the Earl of Zetland KT, Grand Master of the Freemasons of England, had been placed to daunt the unruly. Everywhere she looked there were arches leading to stone corridors and what little light the heavily leaded windows allowed glinted on the brass of commemorative tablets. She sniffed. There was a smell, not strong enough to be called a stench, which pervaded the entrance hall and, one could be reasonably sure, the rest of the building. It was a smell made up of disinfectant, of stale food, of the bodies of those who had once been patients and were now clients, of urine and of dust, of the living and the dead; it had permeated the walls, and would remain until those walls were rubble. It seemed to Sarah that any people – inmates or staff – who breathed that smell day and night for more than a couple of months, though they had been healthy before, would soon sicken; she was glad and grateful that she had been able to leave Jonathan in the car with Wendy.

Within a booth of iron mesh, glass and wood set just inside the door a shutter opened and the receptionist said, 'What do you want?'

'I want to see someone.'

'Who?'

'I don't know who. I was hoping you'd tell me.'

The receptionist said, 'Sorry. I don't do enquiries. You

should have phoned Administration to make an appointment before you set out. That's the usual thing.' And closed the shutter.

'I've come rather a long way. It's a three-hour journey.' The receptionist's manner was hard – Sarah supposed it would have to be – but she did not seem to be a cruel woman; the three-hour journey caused her to waver. Sarah swiftly put in the clincher. 'I've got a baby in the car.'

Even a baby in a car park can melt the carapace of a woman of middle age, and the receptionist was, after all, in one of the caring professions. She opened the shutter again. 'What's it about?'

'I'm trying to track down someone who used to work here. As a cleaner.'

The receptionist grunted. 'Well, at least that's a good start. You might get somewhere. They wouldn't be so free with their information if it was a patient. When was she here?'

'Late nineteen-forties.'

There was a silence. Then the receptionist closed the shutter again and put out her hand towards the telephone as if about to summon assistance. Sarah tapped on the glass, and said, 'Please! I know it sounds odd. Let me explain.' Even the explanation, she realised, was bound to sound a little odd. 'I'm at the end of a sort of trail, and it's led me here.'

The receptionist considered this statement, then nodded, and Sarah began to tell her story. After a short while the Receptionist opened the door of her booth, pushed out a stool for Sarah to sit on and came out of the booth to join her, and shortly after that Wendy came in, worried, with Jonathan who had become unhappy at his mother's absence, and then Wendy went back to the car for the thermos and picnic-basket, and the three women had tea with tuna-and-mayonnaise sandwiches while Jonathan pulled at his bottle.

When Sarah had finished her story, the receptionist nodded again sagely, wiped her mouth with the back of her hand, and said, 'It's not much good sending you to Administration. They wouldn't be able to deal with you at all; it's quite out of what they're used to. Let me have a think.' So she had a think, while Sarah and Wendy waited, and then she said, 'It's a question of records, you see.'

'I thought hospitals were good at that kind of thing. Medical records.'

'It's not so much medical. It's mental here; that's different.'

'I thought they kept everything.'

'There you've put your finger on it. You keep everything, and you might as well keep nothing. It's all to be found, but you can't find it. Leave aside the mice.'

Wendy said, 'What about the human memory? That's not a bad form of record-keeping.'

The receptionist said, 'Right! Got it!' went back inside her booth, picked up the telephone and dialled an internal number. 'Fay? What time does Rupert go off duty? Can I have a word? . . . Rupert, it's Eileen at the main entrance. I've got a lady here I'd like you to talk to. Will you come by on your way out?' She put the phone down again and said, 'Rupert's your man. He'll be down in ten minutes,' and since there was no tea left in the thermos, and they could all do with a drop more, sent Wendy across to the canteen for a refill. During all this time nobody else had come into the entrance hall, and Sarah concluded that the patients of long-stay mental hospitals receive considerably fewer visits than those who can be relied upon either to get better or to die within the year.

Rupert was a man in late middle age, high-cheekboned and serious; he looked like a University Extension Lecturer. 'Forty-six to forty-eight?' he said. 'You're not asking much, are you? I was only twelve in forty-eight, and I'm one of the longest-serving here. A cleaner! And just a temporary cleaner, not one of the permanent staff! There's nobody would remember her.'

'I thought . . . if there was an old staff register with addresses. She must have lived somewhere in the town. Perhaps she had family here. Reeves. Doris Reeves.'

He shook his head slowly. 'You can't keep everything. Addresses of temporary cleaning staff! You're not talking the language of priorities, Mrs Arnott.'

Sarah had heard so much about priorities already, particularly from the Inspector, that she was beginning to resent them, but she bit her lip and kept silent.

Eileen said, 'Who'd know? Somebody must know. I thought you'd know.' Once Eileen had left her booth and accepted tea and sandwiches, she had committed herself to the enquiry, and was not willing to see it fizzle out. Also Rupert had been brought in at her suggestion. If he failed, she had failed. 'Give him time,' she said to Sarah. 'He'll come up with something, given time, always does. He's not a negative person.'

'Reeves . . . Reeves. . . . Wrong sex, wrong occupation. Now, if you'd said Derek Reeves. . . . Though he did do cleaning. Did a bit of everything – ran the newspaper trolley, helped in the dining room and with the ablutions, cut the grass. A very present help in trouble was our Derek to the staff generally, at least in my time. There always is one, of course. More than one often, thank God. Not that I approve of it, mind. It's the trusty system really – makes us more like a prison.'

'Who's Derek Reeves?'

He corrected her. 'Who was Derek Reeves. He's gone now.'

'Dead?'

'Resettled six years ago and therefore out of our ambit. Though I do still go in and see them from time to time.'

'Them?'

'We don't resettle individually if we can help it – receipe for disaster. Derek's one of a group of four, living together in a terraced house with a garden. Idyllic, really; we had a lot of complaints. But that group's been accepted, largely due to Derek; it's one of our successes. You might say our only success.'

'Will you please tell me who Derek Reeves is?'

'I do ramble on, don't I?'

And Eileen confirmed it, 'He does ramble on.'

'It's my age. After fifty, we become verbose – verbose or morose: it's one or the other, and I prefer the first.' Sarah closed her eyes and Jonathan, catching the vibes again, gave an angry cry and began to punch the air in front of him, so that he had to be picked up and rocked by Wendy. Rupert said, 'You want to know about Derek Reeves?'

'Please.'

'He was a patient, as you've gathered, already here when I joined. He'd been admitted as a child back in the late thirties; I don't know why, since he wasn't what they used to call "feeble-minded". Maybe he'd had learning problems. That would have earned him his first label, "backward"; there wasn't such a thing as dyslexia in those days. Backwardness would have led to disruptive behaviour. Second label, "beyond parental control". After that there'd have been offences against property, bring him into the Courts – arson probably; it usually was arson tipped them over the edge. Not that he had any parents now, I remember – came from an orphanage, I think. Shouldn't have been in here, but the authorities didn't know what to do with him. They still don't; we still get these cases when Care breaks down and the Social Services give up. Where was I?'

'Rambling on,' Eileen said.

'Derek Reeves.'

'Well, as I said, he was here when I joined. That was in

nineteen-fifty. He was in a funny state then, very withdrawn, not that I noticed him all that much; he was just another problem patient to me. I was still trying to find my own way around, wondering whether idealism would withstand the impact of reality, if you follow me.'

Wendy said, 'I follow you very well.' Jonathan was quiet now and she returned him to his pushchair.

'There had been someone used to visit him. She'd stopped coming. That was the reason he was withdrawn.'

'Doris.'

'I don't know anything about her working here as a cleaner. It's possible. That kind of job, it's local recruitment.'

'It's the same name. Can't be coincidence.' Sarah turned to Wendy. 'But he'd come from an orphanage. His parents were dead.'

Wendy said, 'Older sister. Has to be. They would have been in the orphanage together, and she'd have tried to protect him. Then he was sent here.'

Sarah said, 'Of course. It was in the log book. She did everything at the village school except help with the annual Sale of Work in aid of Barnado's. She never stayed for that.'

'Blamed them for Derek?'

'Right!'

Rupert said, 'Are you there now? – where you're going. Have you found what you came to find? Or do you want me to ramble on a bit more?'

'What happened to change him from being a problem patient to a very present help in trouble?'

Eileen said, 'I expect Rupert happened. That's the usual case.'

Rupert said, 'I'm afraid I don't know what happened. Institutionalisation, Mrs Arnott; it's a funny thing. You think it's imposed on the patients. It's not imposed. It's organic. It's the way they live, the only way they can live, the way to survive. They accept the *mores* and the norms of the institution, and to do that they have to forget their own. They learn to understand the system and consequently they don't understand any other system. The system demands that they become obedient children, and so they do. People can be swallowed up here, and disappear as people; they melt into the mass. But just a few – the more intelligent ones, the ones like Derek who should never have been here in the first place – they find their individuality within the system. And he did; I don't remember how. Came out of his withdrawal and learned to play the game by our rules. By the time he left us he was one of the most popular people in here.'

'You've no idea why?'

'I think that in Derek's case it would have been a response to need. How old would he have been back in forty-eight? Early twenties? – he's early sixties now. Somebody – his sister, you say – had been coming to see him regularly?'

'Three times a year. Every school holiday. Working here maybe. Staying in the town almost certainly.'

'And then she stopped coming, for whatever reason?'

'She was dead.'

'Did he know that?'

'No, he wouldn't have known. She just stopped coming.'

'So he felt betrayed. It would have come out in violence for a while, I expect; that would have been before I got here. Then withdrawal as the anger went inwards against himself. Bereavement . . . you think it lasts for ever, and then someone needs your help, and you give it; it might have been a child or someone severely handicapped. Up to that time there'd still have been part of him not accepting, a part still attached to the outside world, to his sister, but now that part was dead and he decided where his future was.'

'St Bardolph's?'

'Until we threw him out six years ago. But Derek was one of the lucky ones. We had time for resettlement training, and anyway the brighter ones went out first.' Rupert shook his head. 'The words we use! "Resettlement Training" . . . "Compatability Groups" . . . We've conditioned them to think and behave like children for years – fifty years in his case – and then we say, "Now you've got three months to grow up," and we expect them to do it. And as the pressure grows to close the mental hospitals, it all gets worse. We're pushing out poorer material in less time, and the rate of resettlement far outstrips the ability of the community to receive them. A few of them are placed in jobs, but they don't keep them. They've no protection outside. One of my lads, Jimmy Morrison, sent out earlier this year, he's no skills to speak of, lives in a hostel on Social Security – he got into the clutches of a gang of twelve-year-olds; they'd go with him to the Post Office when he collected his giro money and take it off him.'

Eileen said, 'You're rambling on again.'

Sarah said, 'But Derek's not like that?'

'No, as I said, he's above the average. He holds his group together. He had a part-time job for a while under one of the schemes, cleaning in a bookshop until it went bust. Nobody buys books these days, not even me.'

'Can we meet him?'

'I don't see why not. I'm just going off duty, and it's on my way. You can follow me.'

As they walked together to the car park, Sarah said, 'Will they be in?'

'They're always in. They haven't anywhere to go.'

There were four of them, Derek, Betty, Noreen and Henry, all older than Sarah's mother; the men shared a bedroom, and so did the women. They kept their house very tidy, very clean and tidy, and this was because, as Henry explained, they each had their own tasks, some to be done every day, some once a week, some twice a week, each on its own day and in its own period of the day, morning, afternoon or evening. They offered cups of tea, and although Sarah and Wendy had already consumed a great many cups of tea that afternoon, it would have been impolite to refuse. So everyone had a cup of tea, prepared by Betty. That was four o'clock tea. Tea as a meal would not be on the table until six; that was when they had their real tea. Today it would be boiled eggs, which Henry would boil, tomorrow ham and salad.

They were greatly taken with Jonathan; they had not had a baby in their house before. All four watched while Sarah made up a bottle for him in the kitchen, and watched while he sucked at it. Meanwhile Wendy went to the loo, and reported later to Sarah that the bathroom was very neat and tidy too, which was much to the credit of the household when one considered that they could not have been expecting this visit. Derek, Betty, Noreen and Henry had not been at all put out by the arrival of their unexpected guests. It was as if they were in perpetual readiness for visitors who never came.

None of the household asked the reason for the visit or seemed to expect there should be one beyond the pleasure of the visit itself, but after the introductions and the feeding of Jonathan and the going to the loo and the consumption of the first cup of tea, seven people and a baby crushed into the small front room of a terraced house, it seemed to Sarah that she had better begin, so she said, 'It's a great pleasure to meet all of you, but we've really come to talk to Derek if we may.' Then she waited for Betty, Noreen and Henry to wander away on other business or for Derek to suggest some other part of the house where they might talk, and Noreen, Henry, Betty and Derek, intrigued by such a promising beginning, waited for her to continue. And time passed.

Rupert said, 'It's a communal household, Mrs Arnott. The concept of privacy doesn't really apply here, any more than it did at St Bardolph's, except in matters of going to the toilet and baths and such. I think the general idea is that anything which affects Derek affects everyone.'

'I'm sorry. Silly of me. I should have realised.' It seemed very odd, and even wrong to Sarah that she should be expected to tell Derek what had happened to Dorrie in front of the others, but she turned to him and said, 'It's about your sister.'

There was another silence. Three at least of the communal household were puzzled. Noreen said, 'Derek hasn't got a sister. None of us has got sisters. We've got nobody. That's why we're here. They put us together.' She turned to Rupert for confirmation. 'If you've got a sister, you go to your sister.'

Betty said, 'If she'll have you.'

Henry said, 'I had my mum and dad come to see me. They came every year from Chester. Then they died and they didn't come no more.'

Sarah said, 'I'm afraid that's what happened to your sister, Derek. She died. Somebody killed her. That's why she never came back to see you. I want to find out who did it. Her body was found this summer on our land.'

Derek got up, left the room, and could be heard ascending the stairs. Again there was a silence, then Wendy said, 'Bit up-front, wasn't it?'

'I couldn't think of any other way to put it.'

Rupert said, 'Up-front was best. He doesn't like lies.'

'None of us has got sisters. What they said when they put us together, they said, "You've got each other."'

Betty said, 'Please may I be excused, please,' and followed Derek upstairs. After a short while she returned and said to Sarah, 'You can come up for a bit.' So Sarah had her private interview with Derek after all, except that Betty remained on guard at the open door of the bedroom.

Derek lay on top of his bed, his jacket on the floor beside it, his face turned to the wall. Sarah stood in the middle of the room looking down at him, wondering how to begin, since she had already said so much, and had expected a response, not to have to start all over again. She said, 'May I sit by you on the bed?' Derek did not reply, so she sat by him.

She said, 'Were you together in the orphanage? Barnado's?' She could feel the bed shaking slightly beneath her. Either she herself was trembling or Derek was nodding his head. 'And then – once she'd left – she found out where you were, and came to see you and to tell you that you weren't on your own? The bed shook again. 'Because she loved you, and wanted to be with you?'

Her voice broke. There were tears in her eyes and her throat was tight. The bed was moving like an earthquake beneath her as Derek sobbed, the backs of his fists pressed into his face and his shoulders heaving. Only Betty seemed unaffected by the emotion, staring across at the two of them on the bed, her face set in concentration, trying to follow and to understand because later they would all need to understand.

'And she came here every year, three times a year? She worked as a cleaner at the hospital so as to be near you? The nodding was almost continuous. 'She was a teacher by then, did you know that? She taught at the school in the village where I live. I've read about her. I've seen her picture.' Someone more tactful or more skilled in consolation might have said that Derek resembled his sister, but Sarah could not, since nothing about this solid and serious sixty-two-year-old man, blubbering now with his face still turned away from her, reminded her of the Dorrie in the photograph. 'She was very popular, Derek. All the children loved her.' Should she tell him about the baby, the dead foetus curled inside his sister's skeleton? No, it would be hard for him to understand, and if understood would only distress him further. 'And then somebody murdered her. I've been trying to find out who did it and why. He may be dead by now: the police think so. But I wanted to know.' She put her hand on his shoulder and slowly his head turned up towards her so that they were looking directly into each others' eyes. 'She would have come back; I know she would. She'd never have left you. She wasn't that kind of girl.'

Derek said, 'She was . . . going to take me away. She promised . . . solemn promise. We was . . . going to be in a house. Not like here. Ours. Our house. Dorrie and me. She said . . . I could do labouring. She said . . . she got it all worked out . . . got a plan. She said I was capable. They made a mistake. Shouldn't be there. We'd be together. Then she never came back . . . and I. . . .' He was crying again. Sarah held him and tried to rock him, but he was rocking himself, his arms clutched tight in front of him. 'I stayed . . . in the hospital.'

Betty said, 'You go downstairs now. We'll come in a minute. We'll wash his face first,' and Sarah kissed the top of Derek's head, got off the bed and went back downstairs, where everyone was having another cup of tea, poured by Noreen.

Shortly afterwards Derek and Betty came downstairs to join the group, and shortly after that it was time for the guests to leave. Hands were shaken all round and pleasure on both sides expressed, and Derek held out his hand to Jonathan, who took a finger, pulled it towards him and seemed, until prevented, about to put it in his mouth.

Derek's finger was returned to him. He looked at it, then stroked it gently, as if trying to impress the experience firmly into his memory. He nodded towards Jonathan. 'We should have one of those,' he said to Betty. 'I suppose it's too late now.'

It seemed to Sarah that she probably now had all the pieces of the puzzle. What remained was to fit them into place.

DREAMS

Sarah telephoned the Inspector's office, and after several hours he returned her call. She said, 'Her name really was Doris Reeves. I've found her brother.'

His voice was both weary and wary. 'Could you put it in writing, please.'

'Another thing. Do you have access to Post Office Savings? – the records?'

'It's confidential. But under certain circumstances, yes.'

'I think you'll find she had a Post Office Savings book. Under her own name. Address probably the vicarage at Radcote. The book itself will almost certainly have been destroyed but the account should still be open, because nobody ever closed it.'

'You've obviously been busy, Mrs Arnott. What are you expecting – hidden millions? They only paid two-and-a-half per cent, those accounts. Even after forty-two years, there won't be much in it.'

'I think you'll find a substantial amount. Four figures anyway.'

'All right. I'll have enquiries made.'

'And at Dr Barnado's, please. There's a Head Office, I suppose. She and her brother would have been at one of their orphanages during the mid to late thirties. His name was

Derek. I imagine that's confidential information too, but maybe not to the police.'

'Maybe not.'

'And one last question for you to consider. If the vicar killed her – if he was the father of the child and that's why he killed her, as you're assuming – why did all the villagers keep *stumm* when your people were asking questions? None of them had any reason to protect the vicar. They didn't like him; he was too High Church for them. If they believed the vicar was the father, those who remembered him would have been delighted to put the boot in.'

'You're irresistible in triumph, Mrs Arnott,' the Inspector said. 'I'll get back to you.'

It was the beginning of November, no frosts yet, but the leaves were turning colour. The nicotiana were still in flower, ragged at the edges if one looked closely, but plenty of colour still there, a cloud of lime green just inside the gate. Clyde was pulling them up.

'Do you have to do that?'

'Got to get the wallflowers in.' He had been in the bottom garden all morning, cutting back the perennials, cutting them down to the ground; he called it tidying. Again there had been some late bloom and certainly foliage, where now there were only brown mounds of earth and sticks. Clyde had said that if it were not done now he would be unable to get onto the ground later. A captious wind had sprung up and now, to prove him right, brought a spatter of rain with it.

'Do you want to come in for a cup of coffee until it blows over?'

'No, thank you, Mrs Arnott. This'll get worse; I'll probably have to leave early. Be a full gale by the evening.'

'How can you tell?' It would be some old piece of country lore, Sarah supposed, something to do with the shape of the clouds or the behaviour of cattle. Or maybe the plants spoke to him as he hacked them about.

'Weather forecast.'

She went back indoors, and shortly afterwards real rain began and Clyde packed up his gear, kickstarted his motorbike and was away early, as he had prophesied, leaving raw earth and no wallflowers where the nicotiana had been.

If there were gales, the leaves would fall soon enough, even without a frost. It was Sarah's fantasy that the house was a ship when the wind was up. Timbers creaked in floor and stair, there were obscure bumps and thumps in outhouses and upstairs rooms, and above all the roaring of the wind itself in the woods just above the house was like the noise of a storm at sea, and if one closed one's eyes one could almost feel the floor move. Sarah enjoyed gales; Simon did not. It was one of the few disadvantages of living in such an isolated place that gales or snow – and most of all snow and gales together – almost invariably led to a power cut, sometimes only of a few minutes but sometimes lasting hours, and once for several days. Simon had no liking for candle-light, not even at the dinner table; he liked to see what he was eating. No electricity meant no television and no hot water, which was insupportable, Simon said, in 1990, and only the British would put up with it. Luckily Simon was away tonight in Locarno, representing the firm at a Euroconference on the Marketing of Vat-Grown Nutrition Products. He was to give a paper on Overcoming Consumer Resistance. It was a real career step for Simon.

Darkness closed around the house. Curtains were drawn, the living room fire, already laid, was lit and took flame at once, crackling and spitting, unaffected by the wind. A pot of tea for Sarah, a meal for Jonathan, at six months old already into yoghourt as well as various disgusting purees, then games with Jonathan on the rug with a fireguard to keep the sparks away.

So the evening passed until Jonathan was put to bed, and

Sarah made herself a poached egg on toast with another pot of tea (since there is never any point in cooking a proper meal just for oneself), and settled down by the fire to re-read *The Nine Tailors*. After a while she became conscious of a banging from the conservatory, which could be clearly heard above the noise of the wind; it was more than a bump, and must be coming from the conservatory door, which had a defective catch and sometimes required locking to keep it closed in windy weather. So she went into the conservatory to lock the door, and saw that there was a light in the lower garden.

The light was down by the ha-ha. It was moving; it must be a torch. Since the building of the ha-ha, there was no longer a gate in the lower garden. Whoever was holding the torch must have come in by the front gate, passed by the house and entered the lower garden by way of the shrubbery. Sarah switched on the conservatory light. The light of the torch in the lower garden went out. The light from the conservatory did not penetrate the darkness of the garden outside, but anyone inside was very clearly lit. Feeling horribly exposed, and walking self-consciously as if on a stage, Sarah locked both conservatory doors. Then she switched off the conservatory light, returned to the living room, locked the door between the living room and conservatory, and wondered what to do next.

Obviously she ought to lock the front door. She found herself reluctant to do so. She never had locked it when left by herself in the house, even overnight; one didn't do that sort of thing in the country; it was townee behaviour. It had been a point of pride with Sarah that she never locked the door. However, on this occasion pride would have to give way to common sense. The keys were on the kitchen table. Having made the decison, she moved quickly to the kitchen to get the keys, and went to the front door to lock it whereupon it opened from the outside, and Jeremy was standing there, still holding the torch.

He was windswept and wet but, being Jeremy, not at all bedraggled. Sarah said, 'I didn't hear the car.'

'I walked over the fields. I'll come in if I may.' He was in already.

'It's late, Jeremy. What do you want?'

'Talk to you.'

'All right, you'd better sit down. Would you like a drink? Coffee?' He shook his head. 'That was you in the lower garden?' He nodded. 'Why?'

'Thought I'd take a look.'

'In the dark?'

'I had my torch. Thought I'd take a look where we found her.'

He made no move to sit down, but was still standing there just inside the door, looking at her. He said, 'You've been asking a lot of questions. Research. A project, you said. We used to do projects at the village school when I was a kid.' Sarah remembered Miss Hedges telling her that Jeremy as a child had always been a little too eager to please. He did not seem very eager to please at the moment. 'You've been doing your project at the school too, as I hear.'

Sarah said, 'Any research I did at the school had nothing to do with you. You were never at school when Doris Reeves was a teacher there, Jeremy. She died long before you were born.'

'My nan was.'

So that was it. 'Yes, they overlapped. And then Doris went to her father's farm and gave her tuition. Your father's farm now.'

'You've been poking into things that don't concern you.'

'Is that your nan speaking, or you?'

'Doesn't matter.'

'Did she send you?'

'Don't be stupid.' Meaning that if she had, he wasn't saying. It was, of course, to old Mrs Potter, not to Jeremy, that Sarah had said she was engaged on a project. It had only been three months ago, but seemed an age.

'Did you put those boys up to burning the Morris Eight? Did you help them?'

'If you like. What's it to you?'

Sarah Arnott, you are alone in the house, with only your baby upstairs. There is nobody to protect you, no way you can summon help. This man is young and strong, much stronger than you are. He has a following in the village; whatever he chooses to do, his word will be taken against yours. He had already committed at least one violent crime, if arson counts as violent. You are in a situation which, objectively speaking, should scare you silly. Why aren't you frightened?

'I don't know,' Sarah thought. 'Perhaps I am, but I don't feel it yet.' She had never imagined that any harm could come from Jeremy, who was the apotheosis of right-living. Yet her reading of the Crime Club stories, as well of the newspapers, had often demonstrated that right-living people were capable of very wrong actions, and that generally speaking more harm is caused by righteous than by unrighteous persons.

Jeremy said, 'You better understand; you better get this in your head. You think you can ask questions, stirring things up, but you don't belong here. We belong here; we live here. Everybody knows us.'

It was not true. The absent Saudi Arabian, the urban overspill, the Yuppy intruders, they did not know the Potters as a family, and the Potters themselves had no real history in the village; sixty-seven years was nothing. But Sarah did not remind Jeremy of this. Jeremy said, 'My gramp's an old man. Had a stroke. Suffered enough. Leave him be.'

'*What do you think about war criminals?*' She saw herself for a moment as she had been earlier, enclosed in the glass box of the conservatory, fully lighted and the darkness all outside, and for a moment Sarah did feel fear. She said, 'You're threatening me, Jeremy?'

'That's right.'

'With what?'

'You're on your own, aren't you? Simon's in London; Clyde told me. Anything could happen. Like, for instance, I'm here now, aren't I, in this house alone with you? And who's to know?' She noticed that he was wearing gloves.

She put out a hand and touched one of them. It was of soft black leather, fitting like a skin, therefore unlined. She ran her fingers over the back of the glove, investigating the texture of the leather. For a moment she imagined it touching her throat. Jeremy said, 'Don't do that.'

'Why not?'

He found it difficult to express what he was feeling. 'Intimate gesture.'

'Yes.' Both her hands now enclosed his gloved hand, front and back, moving over the soft black leather, enjoying the feel of it, touching and stroking. Sarah remembered Lily Partridge in Cumbria, washing her hands in invisible water, trying to wash away guilt, remembered Wendy's convulsive wringing of her hands in the vicarage garden as she confessed to her indiscretion about the car, but what expressed embarrassment and remorse when one moved one's own hands against each other in such a way became altogether different when Jeremy's gloved hand was between; it became sensuous, both creating and expressing a sexual tension between them.

The lights flickered, and went out.

Jeremy's head jerked sharply. 'Jesus!' Sarah thought, 'He's more scared than I am. Much more. He's psyched himself up to come and frighten me off, but he doesn't know what to do if I won't frighten.' She realised that Jeremy's not knowing what to do might be far more dangerous than if he had a definite plan, because he might easily blunder into doing more damage than he had intended, but what she said was, 'Power cut. We can get some candles if you like, but there's plenty of light from the fire.'

One of her hands still held his. She drew him with her, unresisting, towards the fire, then stopped and faced him again. He was silent, the threat and bluster quite gone out of him. Power cut. He was staring at her, unable to speak, the flames of the fire reflected in his eyes. Sarah said, 'Your grandfather didn't kill Doris Reeves, Jeremy. I know who did. It wasn't him.' Then she put her hands up to his face, one on each side, and bent it towards her, and kissed him on the lips. 'You can go home now. You don't have to worry,' she said. 'There isn't going to be a scandal.' And dropped her hands.

The dismissal was beautifully done. It was like Candida with Marchbanks. Sarah was pleased with herself. The effect it had on Jeremy, however, was the opposite of what had been intended. He continued to gaze at her, the flames still dancing in his eyes. Sarah had often noticed his eyes, which were brown with gold flecks. Gold and brown were Jeremy's colours, the colours of early autumn; his eyelashes were golden brown and there was a glint of golden stubble on his cheeks and chin. His gaze was direct, almost considering. Sweat had formed on his upper lip. He said, 'If you don't mind, Mrs Arnott, I'd rather stay here with you for a bit.' Then he put his left hand in the small of her back, his right under her chin, which he tilted upwards, and then he kissed her.

Roughly at two in the morning, as was usual with him these days, Jonathan woke and started to cry. Sarah said, 'Sorry about this. I should have warned you,' got out of bed and went to her child. He would need to be changed, which would be difficult if there was still no electricity, and then there would have to be a good forty minutes of cradling and soothing before he went back to sleep.

The lights were working again, and she had changed Jonathan when Jeremy came to join them, unselfconsciously naked. He took Jonathan from her, cradled him and rocked him, walking round the room and making little crooning noises while his genitals knocked against the sides of his thighs. 'Bye, Baby Bunting! Daddy's gone a-hunting,' Jeremy sang, and Jonathan snuggled into the golden fuzz on Jeremy's chest, and very soon went back to sleep and could be settled into his cot.

Sarah said, 'Is that the time? Won't you be missed at home?'

But Jeremy had sent his wife to spend the night with his parents.

'Are you telling me that you knew this was going to happen?'

He was shocked by the suggestion. 'Of course not. But I'd no idea, you see. I knew I had to scare you off, but I didn't know how I was going to do it. Usually I've got a plan for everything, but this time I thought I'd better play it by ear.'

'And?'

'I thought . . . if things got out of control, and I went too far . . . I mean, if I'd ended up actually hurting you, that sort of thing, I didn't want Jean involved.'

'Well, it did go out of control in a way.'

He grinned. 'You could say so.'

'Are you going to tell her?'

He considered the question. 'Not immediately. I will when the time's right. I think you've got to tell the truth in marriage, at least about this kind of thing. I think that's important; all the books say so. And anyway I shall feel better.'

Since there seemed to be very little point in Jeremy's walking back across the fields in darkness when nobody expected him at home, they returned to bed. Jeremy said, 'Are you going to tell Simon? I ought to know because it's bound to affect our professional relationship.'

Sarah said, 'No, I don't think so. It would be much too complicated to explain. You and I won't be doing this again, though. You do understand that?'

Jeremy did understand and thought it entirely proper, on which understanding they made love once more and then both went back to sleep.

The ghost of Doris Reeves came to Sarah in a dream and said to her, 'I had to be with Derek; that was the point of it. I had to get him out of that place. They didn't pay much at the school, and cleaning was worse. I never spent any money on myself, not if I could help it, unless you count the car, and I had to have the car to get to Leominster. I had a savings account and I used to put a little away every week, but it didn't grow, not enough, not enough for a house, and we had to have a house to be independent. Giving that bloody girl extra lessons, that was for the money. She took no interest.'

'And then it stopped.'

'Told her father she wasn't learning anything. She didn't want to learn. She wanted me out of there; that's what she wanted.'

'Because of Tom?'

'Tom Potter. He was the labourer, used to live in at the farm because there wasn't room with his dad and mum. When I started with Eva it was winter, and the farm's two miles from the village. I used to walk out after school, partly to save petrol and partly because my own car used to break down often. If the weather was rough, which it usually was, old Mr Barton would say, "Drive Doris home, Tom, will you?" so that's how I got to know him. And after a bit, one evening, he had a reading book hidden in his overcoat pocket and a notebook and some pencils. He stopped the car before we got to the village, and he hummed and hawed, and he said he'd never been much of a one for English at school, but he'd come to recognise he'd need it if he was going to better himself, and he couldn't afford to pay much, but would I give him half an hour afterwards whenever I went to

Eva? He called it "English", but what he meant was reading and writing; he was near-illiterate really. And as for paying me, I don't think he ever meant to do that if he could get away without. But I remembered Derek, you see. Derek wasn't backward; he just needed proper teaching; I could have done it, and I would, once we were together. So I had a fellow-feeling, you could say, for Tom, and I taught him for nothing, what I could in the time, which wasn't much.'

'And one thing led to another?'

'That's right. The weather got warmer; the nights got longer. There was plenty of other work for Tom, leave out driving me home. So we used to meet where we could, outdoors, well out of the village, usually on a Sunday. And like you say, one thing led to another. You couldn't trust Tom to pull out once he'd got carried away. Anyway, I got carried away myself. He was all golden brown, and he had legs on him and a chest like . . .'

'I know.'

'That's right. You do.'

'And Eva found out? Guessed? Saw you?'

'Never saw us. Nobody saw us. Guessed. She was only fourteen but she had instincts, and she was hot for Tom – hot for any man maybe, but he was the nearest; she was like a ripe pear; she oozed if he squeezed her.'

'And he did squeeze her?'

'Couldn't avoid it. She had the run of the farm, and wherever he was there she'd be – in the cowshed, in the fields, mucking out the pigsheds, if he was there she'd find him and press herself up against him. I don't blame Tom. She was only fourteen, but her tits were bigger than mine. And he was ambitious. But by then I was pregnant.'

'So was she.'

'Came later. She intended it, of course. Mine was accidental. But she wanted Tom, wanted him for herself, wanted him to keep, and that was the easiest way to get him. It was the only way, as a matter of fact. Old Barton would never have allowed it otherwise, but as it was he had no option. And as for me, well I had a bit of a think.'

'Yes.'

'I never wanted to marry Tom, didn't know what to do, to tell you the truth. There wasn't room in my plan for him. I wouldn't have asked him for money either, not even maintenance, not when he was just a farm labourer, because I knew he hadn't got any, no more than me. But when he told me we'd got to stop seeing each other and I got it out of him why . . . then that was different. He owed me. Tom said, "Where can I find that sort of money?' I said, "You'll have to get it from her father," and he did. He didn't care about Eva; he knew bloody well I was worth three of her. But he wanted the farm.'

'You didn't get enough from Tom to buy a house.'

'No, but I was on the way. And what I thought. . . . Me being pregnant . . . I hadn't planned it, but it was bringing me money; it was a way to get what was needed . . . what was needed for me and Derek. And I thought, "It's all I've got. I have to use it. I've got a child coming – should be a good one, because I'm not rubbish and Tom, well Tom was a real looker. Who do I know who wants a child?" There were three childless women in that village, three women who loved children and been denied. Two of them I knew, knew them well; I knew what they wanted. Charis, who'd never been married, and Lily Partridge, whose husband wouldn't give her kids, wouldn't even go to bed with her, make love, any of that – wouldn't or couldn't; he said it was religion, but he may just have been a fairy.'

'And the woman at the Manor?'

'Husband killed in the war. I didn't know her more than to speak to, but she used to come to the school and help out sometimes hearing the Juniors read, and I'd see the hunger.'

'So you took money from all three.'

'One wouldn't have been enough.'

'Promised each of them the child.'

'Said I'd come back at the beginning of the autumn term and bring it with me. Hand it over once it was weaned, proper adoption, all legal. Said I needed the money to help me through the birth – baby clothes, pram and all that – expensive business.'

'And none of them knew about the others.'

'Had to be secret. Charis, and Lily Partridge raised the money how they could; I don't know how. I got more from the woman at the Manor.'

'Did you ever intend to return with the child?'

'Would have been embarrassing with the three of them. Judgement of Solomon. I might have if there'd been only one. I don't know how I would have felt once it was born. I love children too, you know.'

'So where were you going to have the child? Not Nottingham?'

'No, I invented all that. I've never been to Nottingham; it just came into my head – Robin Hood and Maid Marian and all that. We were Londoners, Derek and me. I was going to Leominster.'

'But you never went.'

'I don't know about that. I was ready to go. Went to bed that night all packed and ready. I was leaving in the morning, going in my car. I don't remember what happened next.'

And Sarah said, 'Thank you, Dorrie. If I didn't already know all this, you couldn't have told me.'

The ghost of the Reverend James Elroy Partridge came to Sarah in her dream, the moonlight glinting on the dome of his bald head. He mopped and he mowed, he gibbered and he groaned, but all his gibbering was gibberish, except for these words which he repeated often, 'Nothing! I knew nothing.' And Sarah Arnott said to the Reverend J.E.

Partridge, 'Thank you, Rev. I know you knew nothing. You can go now. *Requiesce in pace.*'

The ghost of Lily Partridge came, and said, 'James knew nothing. He was drugged, as Dorrie was,' and Sarah said, 'I know. I've told him to rest in peace.' And Lily said, 'It was in the cocoa. I had been prescribed barbiturates to make me sleep. You understand that I could not take life, not a human life, but Charis crushed up the tablets in a pestle and gave them to me as powders to mix in with the cocoa, both for Dorrie and James, and I did, and they drank the cocoa and noticed nothing, and went to bed as usual.'

'So there was only enough to put Dorrie to sleep, not to kill her. Which means that since she was buried on a hill, and forty-two years of rainfall drained through the soil, there wasn't enough of a residue for the Forensic people to notice.'

'I know nothing about that; I'm not supposed to know anything about that. When Dorrie and James were both sound asleep I went to Charis in her cottage, and she came with me to the vicarage and went alone up to Dorrie's room, and there she smothered Dorrie with a pillow like the Little Princes in the Tower. The princes were innocent, of course, but Dorrie was evil. We had believed her to be good – Charis particularly had believed this – but we had been mistaken in our belief. It was an evil act, betraying an evil nature, to deceive three women, childless as we all were, by promising a child.'

'Children are given by God.'

'This would have been given by God. A precious gift, given by God to Dorrie, then through God's grace from Dorrie to me – or to Charis, of course. Or Mrs Winterson. Particularly to me, whose need was so very great.'

'Your husband couldn't consummate your marriage, was that it? He wasn't attracted to women?'

'Or to anyone in that way, I think. I should not have agreed to marry him if I had known, but it was possible that he himself did not know until the occasion demanded it. He had kept himself chaste, you see. He had thought of chastity as his Christian duty, but as I now realise, it had really been more of an inclination. He had always been High in matters of ritual, and after the honeymoon – perhaps as a consequence of it – he became more and more convinced of the necessity of a celibate priesthood. I had no option but to respect that, but it was a source of grief. It affects everything, you see, the sexual congress of a marriage. Without it, the companionship goes, respect, sharing, certainly any love. Only habit remains. I told James that I had become an empty vessel, which could hardly be the intention of a loving Creator, but he explained that there were some whom the Creator reserved for a nobler purpose. He meant himself, of course, not me.'

'Did Mrs Winterson have any part in what happened?'

'No, no, why should she? I hardly knew the woman. Charis and I were friends; she was my only friend. Dorrie was foolish as well as wicked to think we should keep such a secret from each other, even though we had been separately sworn to secrecy. Mrs Winterson became very depressed in the autumn when Dorrie did not return, and made away with herself. I can hardly blame her for that, since I have now done the same.'

'You drank your bedtime mug of cocoa, took sleeping tablets, and then smothered yourself. It's true you used herbal tablets from the health food shop instead of barbiturates, and a plastic bag not a pillow, but really you were re-creating the way Dorrie died.'

'You may think so if you wish. In fact it was the most convenient method, given my circumstances, and made the least trouble for others.'

'And when Dorrie was dead?'

'Charis come down to me, where I was waiting in the

kitchen. She said we must move the body quickly while it was still warm and could be manipulated. We stripped Dorrie of her nightie, wrapped her in James's overcoat and placed her in the back of her own car. Nobody in the village had television in those days; they were all in bed by eleven-thirty; there was nobody to see us. I drove the car out of the village to the pumping station where Garbett's pasture ends at the road. We had a spade in each hand and carried Dorrie's body between us uphill in the dark for half a mile to a spot just below the Barn – where your house is now. It was very difficult at first, but the spades kept us from falling over and one's eyes adjust. Charis said we must try to leave the ground looking undisturbed, so she cut turves and then we dug a grave and put Dorrie in, lying flat. I said she must look upwards, not down into the earth. However evil her intentions had been, she might still find redemption. Then we covered her, stamping the earth as firm as we could, and put back the turves and stamped on those, and left her. I heard the church clock strike four as we reached the car.'

'And next morning the car was still at the vicarage and the suitcases were still in her room.'

'You imply that James must have known what happened.'

'Guessed. That something happened. He wrote the epitaph on the back of the car.'

'He knew and did not know. He did not choose to know. I told him that I had bought the car with my own money, left to me by my grandmother – what was called a nest-egg in those days. My grandmother, whose own marriage had not been happy, believed that every woman should have under her own control enough money to enable her to leave her husband. It was a hundred pounds, not quite enough to allow me to leave James, even if I'd anywhere to go, but enough for Dorrie – enough, as I'd thought, to buy me a child. I told James I had paid thirty for the car. The two suitcases were kept, taken with us when we moved to our next parish, and then went with their contents for jumble.'

'And you burned the Post Office Savings Book.'

'Yes. That was how we learned of Mrs Winterson's involvement. There were two items of a hundred and fifty pounds in addition to the sum Charis and I had contributed. One of those would have had to come from the father of the child. There was only one other childless woman in the village who could have given the other.'

'It must have been a temptation to take the money back.'

'It was no temptation. Even our own money was not ours once we had given it away, however mistakenly. We were engaged in an act of justice, not of theft.'

'A hard kind of justice.'

'She was spitting in God's face. Charis, being a heathen, would put it in a different way, but our feelings were identical. Dorrie had been given the gift of a child, and used it first for blackmail and then for fraud. How would the child have grown, beginning in such a way? What begins in evil, ends in evil.'

'Vengeance is *mine. I* shall repay, saith the Lord.'

'We were acting as His agents in this matter.'

And Sarah said, 'Thank you, Lily. If I didn't already know all this, you couldn't have told me.'

Miss Hedges said, 'Pretty close. It was Ovaltine, not cocoa. And the grandmother's nest-egg was a flight of fancy on your part, wasn't it?'

'Deduction. She must have had a bit of money tucked away somewhere. She couldn't have asked her husband for it.'

'It was seventy-five pounds, not a hundred. She had a couple of pieces of jewellery – a brooch and a ring – and sold them. For the rest, what she told you in Cumbria was true. She raided the church expenses and paid it back gradually before the annual audit.'

Taking Miss Hedges for an outing had not been as simple

as Sarah had at first thought. When someone has lost the use of her legs, the process of getting her out of a wheelchair and into a car and later back again becomes complicated in unanticipated ways, and although Sarah had realised that she might need help and had enlisted Wendy, two people had turned out to be of less use than one, only getting in each other's way, with a danger of edginess. However, Miss Hedges had not lost her talent for cogent and forceful instruction, and the thing had been done.

Then, since an outing should *be* an outing and Miss Hedges had not set foot outside the Home for six years, they had taken the scenic route and visited Charlecote House near Stratford-on-Avon before returning to Garbett's Barn for tea. Now they sat, the three of them and Jonathan, in the conservatory, looking out over the fields and the village below. 'And that's your ha-ha,' Miss Hedges had said. 'What a lot of trouble that has caused, though I'm bound to say I don't regret it.'

'You asked me to tell you whodunnit. But you knew whodunnit. You dunnit.'

'I'm a teacher. I ask students to tell me what I already know. It gives me pleasure when they come up with the right answer. Have you informed your Inspector?'

'Not yet.'

'Pity! I was expecting him to stroll out of your downstairs lavatory with a pair of handcuffs. Still,' Miss Hedges nodded at Wendy in a friendly way, 'you've taken the precaution of having a witness to my confession.'

Wendy said, 'That wasn't why I came. I'm here to help with the wheelchair.' She took another slice of cake. 'And for the tea, of course.'

Sarah said, 'If you hadn't pointed me towards the Morris Eight, I wouldn't have got anywhere.'

'No. The car was all that was left, and if anyone had become suspicious at the time, it couldn't have been explained. Dorrie's things – clothing and bits and bobs, nothing of any value or significance – they were all dispersed long ago. Jumble mops up the past. But the car was the loose thread which would unravel everything if you pulled it, because without it how could she have left the village? I didn't know about the epitaph, just as I didn't know Tom Potter was the father. Dorrie knew how to keep secrets. She miscalculated on just the one. Too clever there maybe, too calculating. She thought the hunger for motherhood was such a private thing it could never be told. She didn't allow for friendship, because she had no friends of her own.'

'Did you know about her brother?'

Miss Hedges shook her head, and the corners of her mouth twitched. 'If I had, she might be alive today.'

'Why did you point me to the car?'

'A lot of reasons. I wasn't aware of most of them at the time. You'd put a stick into the mud and the bubbles came up; some took longer than others. At first, I just wanted to see Lily again. It had been so long. What we'd done – what I'd done with her help – had been a kind of poison to our friendship; I'd been glad to see her leave the parish with that Popish dolt of a husband, and she'd been glad to go. I thought, "I want to see you again, Lily Partridge, before I die, and my gut tells me that you want to see me. Once you hear I'm stuck in a home, you'll come." Self-pity, you see: it lurks in us all. So I set you on to find her. And you did.'

'And she killed herself.'

'Yes. Frightened. I should have known. I remembered the laughter and the closeness and forgot her lack of courage, which had been one of the reasons she'd needed me as a friend – to protect her. I failed in that at the end.'

'And the other reason?'

'A tidying instinct. When you come to the end of your life you want things tidy. They aren't, of course, but one can create the appearance of it.'

'And?'

'Boredom. Have you any idea of the boredom, Sarah

Arnott, the soul-killing boredom of a life spent in that place, being helped to get up in the morning, sitting all day in that front room with the others, being helped to go to bed, to the lavatory, day after day after day, summer and winter, rain and shine? If my mind had gone, my memory, my capacity to reason and to rage, it would be bearable. They haven't and it isn't. But imagine . . . a trial . . . newspaper publicity . . . to be the centre of attention for a month or so.'

'And afterwards?'

'Prison. How could it possibly be worse than what I have already?'

There was a silence, broken only by Jonathan, who was beginning to resent being left out of the conversation. Then Wendy said, 'But Sarah won't tell. You know she won't.'

'I could confess.'

'Would they believe you? Would they care?' And another longer silence.

Sarah looked sideways at Miss Hedges. She had her chin up, staring angrily out at the view, and tears trickled slowly down her cheeks. She said, 'Will you continue to visit me now that your investigation is over?'

'Sometimes. When I can. Not as often as I should.'

'There's no should about it, Sarah Arnott. If should's the only reason, don't come. You'd probably better take me back soon, or we shall upset the arrangements.'

When they had returned to the Home and the complicated process of getting Miss Hedges out of the car and into her wheelchair had been completed, she said to Sarah, 'Do you know why you invented the grandmother and the nest-egg?'

And Sarah said, 'Yes, I think I do.'

CODA

In March 1992, when Jonathan was just two years old, Sarah left Simon and went to live in London, staying at first with her mother until she had found a flat of her own. Sarah had known that this was what she intended ever since the night she had spent with Jeremy: the question had been when to do it. She did love Simon, at least she supposed she did; she was fond of him and used to him. And she did greatly prefer living in the country to living in London. But in the end, as the Inspector might have said, she had to talk the language of priorities, and Sarah's priority was freedom. She and Jonathan could not continue to live in Garbett's Barn on their own, because freedom entailed self-reliance, which required finding a way to earn her own living. She could not do this from a large house set among fields, eight miles away from the nearest town, unless she were to take in paying guests during the summer, which was not at all her kind of thing. Instead her mother who, as a Senior Talks Producer, was a person of some influence at Broadcasting House, found her a part-time job as a researcher in radio documentaries. Sarah could not take Jonathan with her on the days she went to work, but there are creches in London if one can pay for them, and after a while she found a friendly and agreeable middle-aged woman, the widow of a bus-conductor, who was happy to come in twice a week.

Simon was more bewildered than angry at the break-up; his mother was both bewildered *and* angry. He failed to see the necessity of such a move, since there was no-one else involved either on his part or hers and generally speaking the two of them got on well enough and better than most. He explained to Sarah that the idea of freedom is an illusion, because no-one is free: he himself certainly wasn't. Sarah agreed with Simon that he was not free and that her own idea that she might become so was probably an illusion, adding that she would not require maintenance except for Jonathan, and that Simon would be welcome to visit them at any time. And for some months he did visit, stopping overnight, particularly at weekends which was when he always had seen them most often, but then he began to put himself about a little more, being no longer obligated to hold off, and the visits became less frequent, and eventually he married a woman older than himself, the ex-wife of someone in the hotel business, and the visits ceased except for an exchange of presents at Christmas.

Garbett's Barn was not difficult to sell, since it stood in countryside still comparatively unspoiled and a recent extension to a motorway had brought it within easy reach of both London and Birmingham. It was bought by a couple from Walsall with children of school age. Unlike the Arnotts they took a keen interest in the life of the village, joined the Parent-Teachers Association at the school, and have presented a silver rose bowl for annual competition at the Flower Show in the Mixed Platter of Vegetables section. Jeremy Potter and Clyde look after their garden.

Old Mr Potter died after a series of strokes. For two weeks old Mrs Potter refused to leave the house, even to attend his funeral, after which she was visited by young Mrs Potter, Jeremy's wife Jean. What passed between them is not known, but old Mrs Potter has now taken to wearing flyaway spectacles and angora sweaters in such colours as raspberry ripple. She is a regular attender at whist drives and participates annually in the coach tours to European cultural high-spots sponsored by the Women's Institute, of which she is a keen and supportive member. Last year she joined the village Fun Run up Gallowstree Hill in aid of the Muscular Dystrophy Association and raised £23.50 in sponsorship. The women of that family age but they do not die. Old Mrs Potter now seems determined not even to age.

When Adrian left the old people's Home at Temple Glazeby, Miss Hedges took against his successor. She became silent and refused to eat. Miss Hedges would have said she was putting an end to her life in the only way open to her, which was to starve herself to death. To the administration of the Home, she was sulking and had gone off her food. An attempt to feed her like a baby met with such a blistering response that a compromise was proposed by which she would eat just enough to keep herself alive and the administration free of blame, but would not be under pressure to eat more. During the hard winter of 1994, Miss Hedges, although she lacked the use of her legs, managed one night to throw her top half out of bed, whereupon the legs followed. The room she shared was centrally heated and therefore unsuitable for her purpose, but she managed by the use of arms alone to crawl to the door, which she opened with her stick, and so into the corridor and a bumpy ride downstairs to the cold lino of the kitchen, where she lay until discovered next morning. She was removed to hospital and died there of a cocktail of ills.

Wendy and Ant were made redundant as they had feared, and their television programme was scrapped. They managed to sell the vicarage at only a small loss and lived for some time in rented accommodation so as to be free to move wherever they could find another job in television, but there were no other jobs in television or in any other field, as it seemed to them, for a couple in their forties. After a period of consistent rejection Ant became depressed and lethargic, so Wendy – encouraged by Sarah with whom she remains in a friendship sustained by letters, telephone and occasional visits – took charge of the direction of their lives. There was still enough capital for a down-payment on a small house in the poorest part of Coventry, and some left over with which Wendy and Ant set up as street traders, selling cheap clothing at country markets. So they persist, sometimes up, often down, but, as Wendy will tell you, still survivors.

And Sarah survives. After eighteen months at Broadcasting House, busy, cherished, respected by her colleagues, she decided that it was wrong for Jonathan to be the only child of a single parent: the emotional weight would be too great. So she became pregnant by a Sound Engineer from Northern Ireland, and gave up her job when she was, like Dorrie, eight months gone. Her mother – predictably – was not pleased.

Sarah has decided that, notwithstanding her mother's expectations, she herself has been right all along about the nature of her talent, that her own precious gift is for motherhood and that the mistake she made was in thinking that she had to be a wife as well. She knows better now. She is perfectly happy for most of the time, making a life for herself and the children, and when she feels any desire to move in a wider world and chaffer in the marketplace, she goes to stay with Wendy and Ant for a while and helps on the stall.

She is a disastrous girl, Sarah Bridges, socially irresponsible, irredeemably scatty. She has an excellent analytical mind but refuses to use it. What can one do with her? I suppose Sarah would say that one shouldn't do anything. If Sarah agreed that anything needed doing, she'd do it herself.

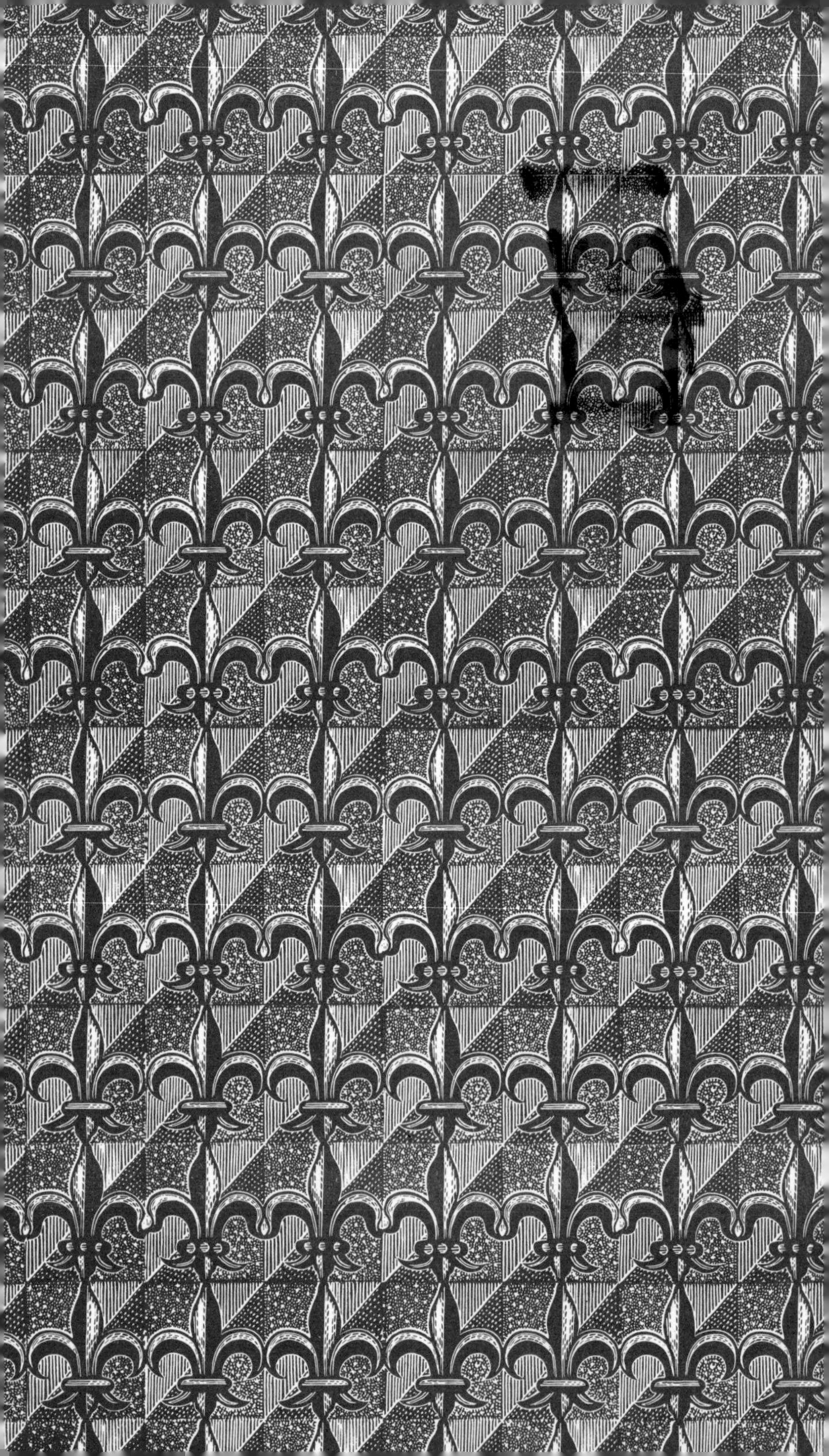